THE BOY WHO WAS A SCHOOLGIRL

by

RUSSELL FRANK

CHAPTER 1

Dan Walter knew he should not be in his sister's bedroom. Alice, his sister, had died two years earlier when she had been run over by a truck on her way home from school. She was just 16. The driver was never prosecuted, claiming that Alice had been larking about on the pavement with her friends and had suddenly jumped in front of him; there was no way he could have avoided hitting her, he said at the inquest. Their mother had been a bit strange ever since, Dan thought. She insisted on leaving Alice's bedroom just as it was when she was killed, almost like it was some kind of weird shrine. She did not actually ban anyone from entering, but she made it clear she did not like it. Sometimes she went in by herself, closed the door and stayed there for as long as an hour. Dan often heard her sobbing.

    Dan checked the time on his mobile: 1535. His younger brother, Toby, would not be back from soccer training until half past five at the earliest. His Mum never got back from the salon - she ran a successful hair and beauty salon in town - before six. He had nearly two hours to himself. He did not really have any plan and he was not at all sure why he was in Alice's room; at least that's what he told himself. Looking around him furtively, even though he knew no one was there, he opened the doors of her wardrobe. All her dresses and skirts were still there. He opened the top drawer of her chest of drawers - it was jammed with a tangle of underwear and tights.

    At the age of 15 he reckoned he was about the same size as his sister when she died. He checked the time again, then, having suddenly made a decision, he swiftly pulled his T-shirt over his head and laid it on the bed. He felt his heart thumping hard. He slipped off his trainers and socks, unzipped his jeans and pulled them off. Standing in just his boxer shorts, he hesitated for a moment. Was he mad? He shrugged, pushed his boxers down to his knees and stepped out of them. He walked, stark naked and feeling weak at the knees, to the chest of drawers and rummaged around until he found a pair of cotton knickers. He felt almost sick with excitement about what he was going to do. He held them up to see which was the front then he put them on, one leg at a time. As he pulled them up, he shivered and felt his willy stiffen; the soft cotton against his privates was a nice feeling.

Next he took out a pair of black tights and sat on the edge of the bed to unravel them. It took him several minutes and much tugging to get them on. How did girls do this? At the open wardrobe he selected a pink cotton dress with a very short gathered skirt. He recognised it as one of Alice's favourites; she wore it often during her last summer. He could not figure out whether he should step into it or pull it over his head. He tried over his head and found it immediately fell into place; there was a zip at the side which he closed with a soft rasp. At the bottom of the wardrobe was a jumble of shoes. He knelt down and found a pair of black ballet pumps which, to his surprise, fitted him perfectly.

  He slowly crossed the room, acutely aware of the skirt kicking out as he walked and his long legs exposed in black tights. He stopped in front of the full length mirror and gasped audibly at his reflection. He was entranced: he really did look like a girl. He had been letting his hair grow for a few months and it was now almost down to his shoulders. He grabbed a hank of it behind his head and pulled it up as if it was a little pony tail: it made him look even more girly. He found a scrunchie on Alice's dressing table and wound his hair through it, then shook his head; he liked the way his new pony tail flicked from side to side.

Most of the make-up on the dressing table had long since dried up, but there was a lipstick with a cap still on it. Dan twisted it off. He had never put on lipstick before and it took him several attempts to get it right. He checked himself in the mirror again, pouted and, giggling, blew himself a kiss with his bright red lips. He looked at his watch again: 1615. He would give himself another 45 minutes to be on the safe side, but he was unsure what to do next.

He sat on the edge of the bed and crossed his legs, thrilling at the soft hiss of his tights. He edged the hem of the skirt up his thighs and admired his legs. Then he stood up and walked around the room, trying to catch glimpses of himself in the mirror. He decided he would go downstairs and get a glass of milk. At the top of the stairs he hesitated, then started down, one step at a time, pleased with the way his skirt billowed out.

For the next 30 minutes he wandered around the house, catching occasional sideways glances at himself as he passed a mirror. At 1645 he returned to Alice's room, stripped down and put her things back exactly where he had found them, then he put on his own clothes and slipped out of the room, closing the door behind him. He felt an overwhelming sense of relief that he had done what he had done without being discovered and he decided, there and then, that he would never do it again. It was too risky; if anyone found out his life would not be worth living.

It was not until he went into the bathroom and looked in the mirror that he realised he was still wearing lipstick. Oh my God, he whispered at his reflection. He rubbed his mouth with a paper towel but it did not seem to make any difference. He washed his face with soap and hot water, but his lips remained stubbornly red. How did women remove make-up? He had no idea. He opened the bathroom cabinet and found, right at the front, a pack of tissues marked "Make Up Remover". It obviously belonged to his mother, he thought; he had never noticed it before, but then why should he? He took out a tissue, gently wiped his lips and was gratified to see that all trace of the lipstick disappeared. He flushed the red-stained tissue down the lavatory.

He said nothing, of course, when his mother came home but she must have sensed something had happened because she kept asking him if he was all right and he kept saying he was fine.

Two days later, a Thursday, Dan was walking home from school. Toby had football training after school every Tuesday and Thursday and so Dan knew he would be alone at home again for several hours, but he told himself that he was definitely not going to go into Alice's room. Definitely.

Half an hour later he was sitting in his bedroom scrolling through YouTube videos looking for advice about make-up. He was wearing a pink T-shirt, a very short, tight black skirt, fishnet tights and Doc Marten boots. Under his T-shirt he was wearing a black bra stuffed with tights. He had been telling himself he would not do it as he arrived at his house, but the minute he had dumped his bag in his own room, he found himself crossing the landing and turning the handle on the door to Alice's room. Then he had opened her wardrobe, just to look…

No matter how many times he promised himself that he was done with dressing in Alice's clothes, that it was sick, that it was too risky, that he was being stupid, every Tuesday and Thursday it was what he did. He even found himself hurrying home on Tuesdays and

Thursdays so that he would have maximum time in Alice's room. After little while he knew her wardrobe as well as his own; he knew which dresses he liked most. Thanks to the hours glued to his laptop screen in the privacy of his bedroom he knew the best way to put on tights (roll up one leg at a time), how to "tuck" (hide his penis between his legs to avoid unsightly bulges in the front of a tight skirt), how to create "smokey eyes" (with eye shadow, a brush and cotton wool) and much more.

He acquired his own make-up at a big Boots in the centre of town which had several self-service tills. After furtively scouting what he needed at the cosmetics counter, he grabbed one item at a time, hiding it in his hand while he queued at a self-service till, then pocketing it the moment he had paid. In this way he did not have to suffer the embarrassment of being served by a female shop assistant. It occurred to him that he could probably nick the stuff, but the prospect of getting stopped for shoplifting lip gloss or mascara almost made his heart stop.

In an effort to find other boys like himself, he Googled "boys in dresses" and found himself entering the labyrinthine world of gender confusion, of boys and girls who believed they had been born in the wrong body, of gender dysphoria, of sexual reassignment. He could not identify with any of it: he did not believe he had been born in the wrong body, he did not want to be a girl and he certainly did not want his willy cut off. He just liked wearing girls' clothes.

He learned, to his amazement and secret envy, that there were dozens of androgynous boys who worked as female models, strutting catwalks in low cut dresses deliberately designed, it seemed to Dan, to show they had no boobs. He got to know their names and followed their careers online. He discovered some dressed as girls even when they were not working, explaining in interviews for fashion magazines that they were simply more comfortable in a frock and heels. This he could understand: boys who looked like beautiful girls deciding that life was simpler if they lived as girls.

Googling "ladyboys" and "shemales" led him, inexorably, to pornographic sites. He was simultaneously shocked and excited watching "chicks with dicks" slipping out of their knickers and playing with themselves while giving blow jobs to some stud prior to being buggered. He had no idea there were so many "shemales" in the world and so many willing to work in the porn industry. Some had large globular breasts, obviously implants, some had pert little tits created by hormones and some had none; some were glamorous, some less so, but almost without exception they could all pass as women. He preferred sites where could see them fully dressed before the action started and he noted that when the action did begin not many of them seemed to enjoy anal intercourse. There were few ecstatic moans; more grimacing and gritting of teeth.

Dan began wondering how many of the women that he passed every day in the street really were women. It was a pleasurable fantasy, perhaps sitting on a bus or out shopping with his mother, to look a girl and wonder if she was, in fact, a boy. Brighton, the city on the south coast of England where they lived, was famous as having the "pinkest" postal code in the country and so it was not unusual to see transexuals and cross-dressers in the street - men who were obviously men doing their best to look like women. But how many were not obvious, he wondered; how many managed to pass convincingly as women?

He had been dressing in his sister's clothes twice a week for nearly two months when his private fantasy world suddenly collapsed in a way he had always dreaded, but hoped would never happen. He was going downstairs in full make-up, including smokey eyes and a bright red lipstick he had bought at Boots the previous day. His hair was in a pony tail and he was wearing a short-sleeved soft fluffy sweater, a little pleated skirt, black tights and ankle-strap platforms with two inch block heels. Alice had once told him they were called "fuck me" shoes; he remembered being quite shocked at the time.

As he reached the bottom step he thought he heard the soft click of a key being inserted in the front door lock. Later he realised he should have run upstairs and shut himself in his bedroom (he might have been able to change and clean off his make-up), but he was transfixed, rooted to the spot, holding his breath and clinging onto the banister with one hand, hardly able to believe what was happening, as the door opened and his mother walked in.

As she caught sight of her son, Sarah Walter felt the blood rush to her head; she thought for a moment she would faint. She knew it was Dan standing in front of her, but the way he was dressed he could have been the ghost of his dead sister.

"Oh my God," she whispered. "Oh my God."

CHAPTER 2

For a moment, neither of them spoke. They just stared at each other in mutual horror. Finally Sarah said, very slowly, "Dan... What... on... earth... do... you... think... you... are... doing?"

Dan did not reply. What could he say? It was all too obvious what he was doing. He began to cry.

Sarah was unmoved by his tears. "What the hell do you think you are doing?" she repeated.

Dan shook his head. He was so ashamed he wished the ground would open up and swallow him. He was sobbing and black streaks of mascara were running down his cheeks. "I'm sorry, Mum," he mumbled. "I'm sorry..."

"You're *sorry*..." Sarah's voice was heavy with sarcasm. How long has this been going on?"

Dan shook his head again.

"I asked you, how long has this been going on?"

"A few weeks."

"How long is a few weeks?"

He shrugged.

"They're Alice's things you're wearing aren't they?" Sarah demanded, although she knew the answer.

Dan nodded miserably.

Sarah felt herself getting angrier and angrier. "How dare you go into her room and root about in her things, let alone put them on?" she shouted. *"How dare you?"*

"I'm sorry, Mum," he sobbed. "I didn't mean anything. I didn't mean to upset you. I really didn't…"

"You didn't think I'd be upset to seeing you walking around in your sister's clothes?"

"I didn't think you'd find out. I don't know why I did it. I'm sorry. I'll never do it again. I promise…"

As Dan pleaded with his mother for forgiveness, she looked him up and down carefully. Once the shock of seeing him dressed the way he was began to wear off she slowly began to realise how convincing he looked as a girl. He did not look like a boy in a skirt at all, he looked like a young girl wearing too much make-up. He looked, in fact, just like his dead sister, particularly as he had let his hair grow in the last few months; it was thick and blond, just like Alice's. It was almost as if Alice had come back from the dead and the thought made her feel faint. She tried to pull herself together by wondering how far he had gone with the masquerade.

"Are you wearing Alice's underwear too?" she suddenly demanded.

Dan hesitated. He thought he could possibly gain a shred of dignity or self-respect if he lied. He shook his head.

Sarah caught his hesitation. She knew him too well. "Show me," she said.

"Mum!" he protested.

"Show me, Dan," she insisted. "Lift your skirt and show me what you are wearing underneath."

Dan sighed, gripped the hem of his skirt with one hand and slowly lifted it. Sarah could see, clearly under his tights, that he was wearing his sister's knickers. She was furious.

"Go to my room and get my hairbrush."

Dan swallowed hard. When he was little his mother had often spanked him gently with the back of her hairbrush. "Mum," he said in disbelief. "You can't spank me. I'm fifteen."

"I can and I will. I am not punishing you for what you are wearing. We'll deal with that later. I'm punishing you for lying; that I can't tolerate. Now go and get it."

Dan knew there was no point arguing with his mother. "Shall I change?" he asked.

Sarah's immediate instinct was to say yes, to get out of those ridiculous clothes, but then she reconsidered. At that moment all she wanted to do was humiliate him for what he had done, for violating Alice's space, and she suddenly thought of a way to do it. "No," she said, "stay as you are."

Dan was surprised. He didn't want to be with his mother dressed the way he was; it felt weird. "Please, Mum, let me change," he begged.

"I said no," she snapped. "What part of no don't you understand? Anyway, why would you want to change? You obviously like dressing as a girl because that's what you've been doing behind my back. Now you can do it in front of me. You should be pleased."

Dan sighed again, turned and went back upstairs. Sarah was surprised to see how easily he walked in heels and how shapely his legs were in tights; any girl, she thought, would be happy to have legs like that. "Come into the sitting room when you've got the brush," she said to his back.

All the thrill that Dan had experienced dressing secretly in his sister's clothes had gone. Now, dressed as he was in the presence of his mother, he just felt stupid. He could not believe his mother was going to spank him. He picked up the brush in her room and noticed in the mirror that his mascara was streaked from his tears. He quickly used one of her make-up remover tissues to wipe his cheeks clean before he returned downstairs.

His mother was waiting for him in the sitting room and held out her hand for the brush, which he gave her. "You're too big for me to put you over my knee," she said, "so I want you to bend over the back of the sofa."

"Please don't do this, Mum," he protested. "I'm a teenager now; I don't want to be treated like a child. I'm very sorry for upsetting you, but I thought you would never find out what I was doing. Honestly. I know it was wrong and I won't do it again. Please let me go and change into my own clothes…"

Sarah shook her head. "You lied to me, Dan. Deliberately lied. There was no need. Now bend over."

Dan could see from his mother's expression that there was no way he was going to dissuade her. As he bent over the sofa he felt his mother flipping up his skirt and winced in anticipation of what was coming. Sarah found herself infuriated by the exposure of Alice's knickers and tights on her son's backside. How dare he! She lifted the hairbrush and brought it down with all the angry force she could muster. Dan yelped in pain and tears started from his eyes. Each time the brush made contact with his backside the pain was worse. "Please

Mum, stop," he gasped. "You're really hurting me. Please stop."

Sarah realised she was going too far. In her fury, she had lost count of how many times she had raised the hairbrush and brought it down again. "OK," she said. "You can stand up now. Don't ever lie to me again or you will get the same treatment, do you understand?"

Dan, still sobbing, straightened up and brushed down the back of his skirt, wincing as he did so. His bum was throbbing and felt as if it was on fire. His mother thrust the hairbrush at him and said "Take this back to my room and come down again straight away."

"I'll change, shall I?" he asked hopefully.

"No, you'll stay as you are."

Dan could not understand what his mother was playing at. If she was so shocked and upset at seeing him in Alice's things why was she not letting him change?

"Actually, while you are upstairs you'd better fix your make-up. It's a mess."

Dan wondered if he had heard right. "What do you mean?" he asked.

"You heard me. Look in the mirror. You've got make-up upstairs, haven't you?"

Dan was embarrassed to admit he had his own make-up but he certainly wasn't going to lie about it. He nodded.

"OK, use it."

He hesitated. "Mum, I don't think this is a good idea. Toby will be home soon. I think I had better…"

His mother snorted. "That's right, Toby will be home soon. That's why I want you to repair your make-up because I want him to see what a pretty girl you are…"

Dan reddened. He was incredulous. "You're not serious,"

"Never more so."

Dan felt himself panicking. "Mum, I can't let Toby see me like this. I just can't. He'll tell everybody. My life will be ruined…"

"You should have thought of that before you started poking around your sister's room. Actions have consequences, you know."

"PLEASE! PLEASE! Please don't make me do this. I beg you…"

Later Dan would wonder why he did not simply defy his mother, go upstairs and change into his own clothes. What could she have done about it? Nothing. But at the time it did not occur to him; he was so cowed by having been caught in a skirt that defiance was out of the question.

He began to cry again. "Why are you doing this to me?" he sobbed.

Sarah snorted. "I could ask you the same question." Her determination to punish him for what he had done was undiminished, but she recognised his fears were justified. "Now, Dan," she said in a slightly kindlier tone, "I can promise you that Toby will not tell anyone because I shall warn him that if word gets out I shall not only put him in a dress but I'll make him go to school in it with a ribbon in his hair. That will stop him. Now stop crying and do as I tell you. Go upstairs, fix your make-up, then come down and I'll give you an apron and you can help me prepare dinner."

    Dan reluctantly did as he was told. He still could not understand why his mother was doing this to him and he dreaded what would happen when his brother came home. He sat at the mirror in his room, cleaned up his mascara and refreshed his lip gloss. It gave him no pleasure to see himself when he had finished; all he could think about was how Toby would react when he saw him for the first time dressed as a girl.

His mother seemed pleased when he got back downstairs. "That's better, dear," she said. "You look nice; you certainly know how to put on make-up, don't you? How on earth did you learn to do it?"

Dan shrugged; it was not something he wanted to discuss with his mother. He sullenly put on the apron she handed him ("You don't want to get any food on your nice top or your skirt, do you?" she had said) and stood at the sink peeling potatoes. Every few minutes he checked his watch; he knew his brother would be home around six o'clock.

At five minutes to six his heart missed a beat as he heard the front door open and slam shut and Toby calling out that he was home. He was still standing at the sink, with his back to the room, when his brother burst into the kitchen.

Toby did a double-take when he saw a "girl" at the sink. He made a face, frowned, and mouthed "Who's that?" to his mother. Sarah smiled; this was the moment she had been waiting for. "Turn round, Dan," she said, "and let your brother see what a pretty girl you are."

Toby's mouth dropped open. "That's Dan?" he asked.

Dan slowly put down the potato peeler and turned to face his brother.

Toby stared at him uncomprehendingly, looking him up and down for a few seconds seemingly unable to believe his eyes, then he began to laugh as if the sight of his brother in a skirt and high heels was the funniest thing he had ever seen in his life.

Dan wanted to step forward and hit him, but restrained himself. Instead he appealed to his mother. "Tell him to stop, Mum, please," and when she just smiled he turned on his brother and shouted "SHUT UP YOU LITTLE SHIT, SHUT THE FUCK UP!"

His mother immediately intervened. "Watch your mouth," she snapped and then added, with malicious intent, "young lady."

This set Toby off again. "Oh my God," he giggled, "young lady. Young lady. My brother's a young lady… oh my God. This is too good to miss…"

He threw his backpack onto the kitchen table, fumbled around inside and then brought out his phone. Dan knew exactly what he was about to do and launched himself at his brother and began grappling with him for it.

Sarah stepped forward to separate them, shouting "That's enough! Stop it you two."

"Tell him he's not to take my picture," Dan grunted breathlessly as he tried to prise the phone from his brother's grasp. "Tell him, Mum. Please."

"Yes. Stop it, Toby. Put your phone away. Now."

Toby grudgingly returned it to his backpack. "I'll get a picture later," he muttered. "It'll be a big hit on Snapchat."

"No it won't," Sarah said firmly. "I'll talk to you later, but I'm warning you now, Toby, that if word of this gets out, you too will be wearing a dress, do you understand? I'm deadly serious. You'll be turning up to football practice in a skirt unless you are careful."

Toby pouted. He wasn't sure he believed his mother, but he did not want to take the risk . He picked up his backpack, took one last look at his brother, smirked, muttered "Freak!" and stalked out.

"Now can I change?" Dan asked. "Please?"

Sarah shook her head. "It's nice having a girl around again," she said.

Sarah recognised it was cruel to make Dan stay in a skirt until his brother came home, but she wanted to humiliate him to the greatest possible extent, not just because she had caught him cross-dressing but because he had violated her memory of Alice. Seeing him dressed in her clothes and looking eerily like his dead sister pained her terribly and sharpened her still raw sense of loss. She also hated the thought of him rooting around in Alice's room, pawing through her underwear and trying on her dresses. Did he have no respect for her, or for her memory?

She wondered how long he had been doing it. He had admitted to "a few weeks", but she suspected it was much longer. There was no way he could be as comfortable in a skirt as he clearly was after such a short time. He even, she noticed with something akin to shock, almost instinctively tucked his skirt under his bottom as he sat down. And how did he become so proficient at using cosmetics?

Sarah stayed up late that night after the boys had gone to bed, with Toby still joshing his brother and asking if he was going to wear a nightdress instead of pyjamas and sarcastically reminding him not to forget to take off his make-up and Dan shouting at him to shut up. Sarah told Dan to replace all Alice's things exactly where he had found them before he went to bed, which he did.

When she finally got to bed herself she found sleep almost impossible. She tossed and turned in her lonely bed, wondering what she should do. Her instincts were liberal. Did it matter if her son wanted to cross-dress? No. What she mainly objected to, and was never going to allow, was that he had been dressing in the clothes of his dead sister. But what were the implications of a teenage boy wanting to dress like a girl? She had no idea.

She remained distracted all next day, spending most of her time in the salon trawling the internet for information about teenage gender issues. By the end of the working day she had decided what she was going to do and she felt curiously excited about it. Most of the town centre shops were open until seven or eight in the evening. By the time she had closed the salon she had made a detailed shopping list of what she would need. She found a perfect dress - a short denim shift - in Gap, then bought underwear, tights, a shoulder bag and a pair of ankle boots with low heels - the kind that every teenage girl in Brighton seemed to be wearing.

  She kept telling herself that what she was doing was for Dan, to help him, to keep his options open. Whenever the thought entered her mind that perhaps she was subconsciously trying to deal with the absence of Alice, she pushed it firmly away.

CHAPTER 3

Everyone had told Sarah Walter that time heals, that, one day, she would get over losing Alice, but she knew she would not. Not a day passed without her thinking of Alice, remembering the way she wrinkled her nose when she laughed, the way she teased her brothers, the crazy things she said, the twinkle in her cornflower blue eyes, her zest for life. Just 16 years old and completely unaware that she was already a beautiful young woman.

She knew she would never forget the moment those two policewomen with long faces knocked on the front door. She was alone in the house, making a cake for Dan's birthday; she was wiping her hands on an apron as she opened the door. They looked at each other; neither wanted to speak. Then one of them said "Mrs

Walter? Mrs Sarah Walter?" and she nodded. She knew it was bad news. She could still recall the entire conversation, word for word, how sorry they were, it was an accident, no one to blame, it had been quick, she had not suffered. She remembered how she had crumpled to the floor and howled like a wild animal, how they had tried to lift her up, but she had told them not to touch her.

She had tried not to lose control as she broke the news to the boys. Dan's face crumpled and tears sprang from his eyes; Toby just went deathly pale. Neither said a word. What was there to say? Then she telephoned her former husband in New York, the bastard who had walked out on his family after admitting he had been fucking his secretary for two years and that she was pregnant by him and that he wanted to move in with her. She could hear him weeping at the end of the telephone, but felt no compassion; she hated him.

They had met at university - Sussex - and fallen passionately in love. Tristram Walter was a year ahead of her; studying economics. He was tall, almost too good looking, funny, casually charming, clever and an all-round sportsman who captained both the University rugby XV and the first eleven cricket team. What was there not to like? He had a reputation as a stud but once he had hooked up with Sarah he swore he never looked at another woman. And why should he? Sarah was a stunning beauty and had abandoned a promising career as a model in favour of studying for an English degree.

They were, without doubt, the University's golden couple, even if they came from different worlds. Tristram's parents lived in a moated manor house surrounded by parkland in the heart of the Sussex countryside; Sarah grew up in a small terraced house in the back streets of Brighton with her mother, who was single and paid the bills by working all hours as a cleaner.

Tristram's friends warned him that Sarah was thick - she failed her degree - but he did not care. Neither did it bother him that his parents made it clear they thought she was not good enough for him. "You just think that because you are both hopeless snobs," he told them cheerfully.

After graduation Tristram joined a hedge fund in the City and quickly began making serious money. Sarah had started training as a hairdresser (somewhat to his embarrassment) but soon found she was pregnant. Alice was born a month after they married at Brighton registry office. (His parents did not attend.) They moved into a large double-fronted Regency house in Kemp Town, not far from where Sarah's sister, Eve, lived with her husband and three young children. The arrival of Dan and Toby put paid to any possibility that Sarah would take up a career as a hairdresser, to her husband's great relief, and she was perfectly happy to give up any thought of work and devote herself to her children.

While Tris was an excellent father he was unable to hide his disappointment, at least to his wife, that Dan, his first-born son, was far from a chip off the old block. Whereas Tris excelled in all sports when he was a boy, Dan was useless at all sports. Worse, he was not in the slightest bit interested. Tris did everything he could to turn Dan into a carbon copy of himself when he was a boy - and failed. When Toby showed some prowess at football, Tris lost interest in Dan and concentrated on encouraging Toby to succeed. Dan was not bothered: he made his mother laugh when told her he would much rather read a book than kick some stupid ball. "Don't say that to your father," she had said, only half joking.

In Tristram's macho world of high finance and risk-taking there was little tolerance for diversity and he made no secret of the fact that he was an unashamed homophobe. He swore he could neither understand, nor abide, "queers" and "poofs". Eve, his sister-in-law, enjoyed pulling his leg and slyly suggesting his views were outrageous for someone who chose to live in a city like Brighton. "You know blokes who bang on about queers the way you do," she once told him, "often only do so to hide the fact that they are queer themselves. Do you think that's your problem, Tris?" "Who said I had a problem?" he retorted.

Despite all this, Sarah thought she had a happy marriage and was devastated when Tristram announced - completely out of the blue - that he was leaving her and the children to go off with his pregnant secretary - "the tart" as Sarah referred to her ever afterwards. The children reacted differently to the news: Alice sided with her mother and said she never wanted to see her father again; Dan was secretly relieved; and Toby was heartbroken.

Shortly after "the tart" had given birth - Sarah was pleased to learn it was a girl because she knew that Tristram would have wanted a boy - they moved to New York. Tristram initially seemed to do his best to stay in contact with the children, but Alice's hostility and the distance caused major problems and his telephone calls and e-mails became less and less frequent.

A canny lawyer friend of Sarah's secured a major financial settlement for her divorce and to the surprise of everyone she bought an ailing hair and beauty salon in the centre of Brighton and turned it into a great success. "Are you sure you are doing the right thing?" her sister had inquired. "What do you know about running a business?" "Nothing," Sarah had replied, "but I'm a quick learner."

The salon was just beginning to turn a profit when Alice was killed. To Sarah's fury, Tristram insisted on attending her funeral and brought "the tart" with him. She spoke to neither of them. "Only the tart could make the day worse than it was," she complained to her sister. "It's hard to believe I ever loved Tristram now that I hate him so much."

Sarah never intended that Alice's room should be left as it was; it just happened that way. Sometimes she got comfort from sitting quietly on Alice's bed and remembering… sometimes, mad with grief, she thought she could hear her daughter's laugh. Sometimes she just sat at the dressing table and examined the make-up scattered all over the table top. The number of times she had had to nag Alice to tidy her room; she never did. Sometimes she just sat there and cried.

The boys, of course, were a great comfort to her - particularly Dan, who was much more sensitive than his younger brother. Sarah told her sister that she would not have been able to carry on after Alice's death were it not for the boys. At least once a week both boys would drop by at the salon after school and get a lift home with their mother when the salon closed. Toby kept his hair very short but when Dan decided to let his hair grow the girls in the salon would tease him gently and offer to style it for him and make him blush. "You could be a dead ringer for Taylor Swift if you'd wear lipstick and a mini skirt," one girl joked. Dan giggled and blushed even more.

Sarah knew there was something going on with her eldest son, but she could not figure out quite what it was. He had changed and not entirely, she thought, just because he was entering adolescence. He had taken to sitting with his knees pressed tightly together, which was strange, she thought, for a boy. At the salon one afternoon she caught him apparently engrossed in a women's fashion magazine and when she asked him what he was reading he was embarrassed, threw it down and said he thought it was a photo magazine. Then one evening when they were sitting down together at home for dinner, she noticed a slight black smudge on one of his eyelids. When she pointed it out he immediately got up from the table and left the room. It had gone by the time he returned. Sarah asked him what it was and he said he didn't know, maybe it was a piece of soot or something.

But Sarah was pretty sure she knew what it was. It was mascara.

CHAPTER 4

Dan was relieved when, on the morning after being discovered in Alice's clothes, nothing was said before he went to school. It was as if nothing had happened. He was kind of sad that his Tuesday and Thursday afternoon adventures were over, but he was also kind of glad that he had been found out. The tension of making sure he was back in his own clothes, make-up removed, all incriminating evidence hidden, by the time his mother or his brother returned home sometimes left him weak at the knees. It was fun while it lasted, but he recognised that it could not go on for ever.

Friday evening they all had take-away fish and chips, as they did every Friday, and still nothing was said, although Toby took every opportunity to whisper "Freak!" whenever he thought their mother would not hear. Dan ignored him. He was surprised that his mother seemed unusually happy, chatting about this and that. She seemed, to Dan, to have completely forgotten the drama of the previous day, or if she had not forgotten she had no wish to resurrect it and for that he was grateful. He assumed he had been forgiven and so when his mother said she wanted him to go shopping with her in the morning he whined "Do I have to?" and when she said yes, he made a face and sighed.

"Why can't Toby go?" he asked.

"As you well know, Toby can't go because he has football. And in any case I need you to come."

Toby smirked. "Yes, freak, I've got football, so you'll have to help Mummy with her shopping like a good little boy, or maybe girl…"

"That'll do, Toby!" their mother snapped. "One more word from you and I'll make you come too, football or no football."

Sarah waited until the morning, and until Toby had left the house, before she dropped her bombshell. "I think it might be easier," she said as Dan helped her clear the breakfast dishes, "if you wore a frock when we go out today."

Dan thought he had misheard. "Sorry?"

"Well, you'll need to try stuff on and it will obviously be easier if you are wearing a dress."

"Mum, what are you talking about?"

Sarah laughed, rather nervously. "Oh I'm sorry, darling. Of course I haven't told you. I've been thinking about what happened on Thursday and I've decided that it would be wrong of me to stop you cross-dressing, if that's what you want to do. My only objection is that I don't want you to borrow Alice's things, so I thought we would go out together today and buy you a whole new wardrobe for you to wear whenever you want."

Dan's mouth dropped open. This was the last thing he had expected and he was not at all sure it was what he wanted. "You want to buy me girls' stuff?" he asked, incredulously

Sarah laughed again, even more nervously. "Well there wouldn't be much point in buying you more boys' things, would there?"

Dan was confused. It had never occurred to him that his mother would suggest such a thing; he had accepted that he would probably never again be able to put on a dress. Now she apparently not only wanted to take him out shopping for dresses, but dressed as a girl. He could not believe it.

"You're not serious."

"Of course I am. I got you some things last night - a sweet little denim shift that you can pull on and off over your head in the changing room…."

"Mum, I can't go into a women's changing room!"

"Well, you can if you look like a girl. And do you want to follow me around looking at dresses and skirts and tops and underwear dressed as a boy? Now *that* would be embarrassing."

"Mum, you don't understand. What if someone sees me?"

"Yes, a lot of people will see you and they will see a very pretty girl."

"You know what I mean. What if I run into someone from school? If anyone finds out I have been going around Brighton in a dress my life will be hell."

"I've thought of that. We won't shop in Brighton. There's a very good shopping mall, West Quay, in Southampton. We'll go there. That's sixty miles away.

The chance of you running into someone you know there is zero."

Dan was exasperated by her refusal to see the risks he would be running. "What about the neighbours? That old busybody next door is always looking out of her window to check what is going on in the street. She's sure to see me and then she'll tell everyone that she has seen Dan Walter leaving the house dressed as a girl. I'm sorry, Mum, I can't do it, I just can't."

Sarah was surprised by his opposition to her proposal. She had thought that he might be excited by such an expedition, but that if he needed persuasion it would not take much to convince him to co-operate. As the hopeful prospect of having another girl - perhaps a girl just like Alice - in the house began to recede, she racked her brains to find a way he could leave the house as a boy but arrive at West Quay as a girl. Obviously he would be very difficult for him to change in the car and impossible for him to do it in a public lavatory… then she got it.

"OK," she said, "this is what we'll do. You'll pack a bag here with everything you need. There are dozens of hotels around West Quay. We'll take a room in a hotel, you can get ready in the room, then we'll go out and shop and when we're done we'll go back to the room and you can change back. How does that sound?"

Dan thought about it. He was bothered by his mother's sudden change of heart; only two days ago she was angry, almost disgusted, to find him dressed as a girl at home. Now she wanted to take him shopping as a girl. What was going on? He had no idea, but the more he thought about what she was suggesting the more thrilling it became. He was fairly sure that he could pass as a girl without too much difficulty and the thought of returning home with his own dresses that he could wear any time he like made his heart race. He tried to think what might go wrong.

"But I'll be seen as a boy when we arrive at the hotel and then if I come down as a girl everyone will know…"

Sarah shrugged. "First of all, what does it matter? Who cares what the people behind the reception desk think? Anyway, you could put on a bit of make-up in the car and tie your hair up in a pony tail before we go into the hotel and they'll just assume you're a girl anyway."

Dan could see the sense of what she was saying, but his mind was reeling. On the one hand he was longing to go along with what his mother was proposing, on the other he was terrified.

"OK," he said at last, "if you're sure it will be all right…"

Sarah beamed. "I'm sure," she said, although in truth she was not at all sure. She was not even sure that what they were going to do was sensible; all she knew was that she wanted it to happen for reasons she was unwilling to confront.

Half an hour later they were in the car on their way to Southampton. Dan was wearing knickers and tights under his jeans, a training bra under his T-shirt and sneakers. In a bag on the back seat was the denim dress, a petticoat, a pair of ankle boots and a shoulder bag containing cosmetics, a hairbrush, tissues and money. His mother had suggested he wear a training bra and a petticoat to "protect his modesty" in the changing room. It had not occurred to him that he would need a handbag until his mother asked him how many times he had seen girls out shopping without one.

Everything went to plan. In the car park of the Premier Inn, close to West Quay shopping centre, Dan put his hair up in a pony tail and, using the rear view mirror of the car, put on lipstick and mascara. He was anxious walking into the reception area with his mother, but no one took any notice of them.

It was not until they got into a room on the second floor that he suddenly got cold feet. As his mother pulled the dress out of the bag and began unfolding it he whispered "I'm not sure I can do this."

She had been expecting a last minute failure of nerve. "Of course you can," she said briskly, "don't be silly."

"No Mum, I can't. Let's go home."

Sarah sighed. "Look Dan, if you don't want to do it, that's fine. Obviously I can't make you. But if you back out now, that's it. I'm not willing to do this again, to make all the plans and come all this way only for you to say you can't do it. I completely understand you are nervous, but I am sure that after a few minutes you will begin to enjoy it. I can also promise you that no one, *no one*, will realise you are a boy…"

"Are you quite, *quite*, sure?" he asked doubtfully.

"Absolutely certain. You know I am right. When you were dressing in Alice's stuff and looked in the mirror did you see a boy?"

Dan shook his head.

"Right!" Sarah said triumphantly. "Come on, let's get you ready. This is going to be fun…"

CHAPTER 5

Sarah had imagined she would need to help her son get dressed and also help him with his make-up, but he would have none of it, picked up the bag and disappeared into the bathroom. While she waited, she sat on the bed wondering what on earth she was doing. She must be mad, she told herself, not only encouraging him on this crazy adventure but facilitating it. She kept telling herself it was nothing to do with what happened to Alice, that it was all about Dan, what he wanted. If he wanted to dress as a girl now and then, why shouldn't he? There was nothing wrong about it; people were relaxed about gender these days.

She thought about calling her sister to tell her what was going on, but decided against it. She suspected she would not approve. Eve, her sister, had three teenage boys who were all mad keen on sport; they were big, strong macho boys who would rather die, Sarah thought, than put on a dress. Dan was different, quite different. There was nothing wrong with being different, was there? She wondered what her ex-husband would say if he knew what was going on. He would be appalled, she thought. Good. As far as Sarah was concerned, her ex-husband forfeited all rights over his children when he buggered off with "the tart" and moved to New York.

She looked at her watch. Dan had already been in the bathroom for 20 minutes. What on earth was taking him so long? "Are you all right in there, sweetheart?" she called out. "Yes," came a muffled reply. "I'll be out in a minute."

When, fifteen minutes later, he emerged, Sarah gasped. "Oh my God," she said, "You look amazing."

And he did. She was unprepared for just how convincingly he could transform himself into a girl, unaware of course that he had been secretly practising for months. He was wearing too much eye make-up for her taste, but no more than many young girls, and she was astonished how well he had applied it. He had even painted his fingernails and had tied his hair back loosely with a blue ribbon that matched his dress.

"Is this all right?" he asked nervously, gesturing down at his dress.

Sarah nodded. "I can promise you, absolutely promise you, that not in a million years would anyone think you are a boy. You look absolutely gorgeous."

Dan smiled and blushed. Sarah delved into her handbag, pulled out a pair of clip-on hoop earrings and gave them to him. "Here, you might want try these."

He took them from her tentatively, stood in front of the mirror and turned his head from side to side to put them on, then shook his head slightly to make them wobble. He grinned. He was obviously pleased with the effect, but his smile faded when she said "OK, are you ready to go?"

"Are you *quite* sure it is going to be all right?" he asked again.

"Yes, I am quite sure, now let's go. Where's your bag?"

"In the bathroom."

"OK, go get it and let's get out of here."

Dan needed all the reassurance his mother could offer him. He knew he looked good, that he could pass as a girl, but he also knew he was a boy and could hardly believe that he could step outside in a dress without everyone pointing at him and shrieking "Why's that boy wearing a dress?" In the bathroom to collect his handbag he urgently needed to pee - his nerves were getting to him. He lifted his skirt and petticoat and pulled down his tights and knickers. It was while he was peeing that he realised he should be sitting down, but by then it was too late. He pulled up his knickers and tights, let his petticoat and skirt drop, then picked up his bag and joined his mother.

He felt his heart beating fast as they stepped into the corridor and headed for the elevator. He was relieved there was no one about. His legs felt weak and he might have turned back if his mother had not gripped his elbow. When the elevator doors opened he saw there was a middle aged man already inside. Again he hesitated but his mother said "Come along dear" and guided him inside. The man smiled and said "Good afternoon ladies" and Sarah almost laughed out loud.

When they reached the ground floor the man stepped to one side to allow them out first. Sarah smiled at him and murmured "Thank you", then took Dan's elbow again to guide him across the reception area. There was a family checking in, but no one paid any attention to the mother and her pretty daughter on their way out.

Dan breathed a sigh of relief when they got to the car. He wrenched open the door, put one foot in and suddenly found his skirt hitched up to his thighs. He looked about him guiltily, quickly got in and slammed the door. His mother had seen what had happened and laughed. "You're going to have to learn how girls get into cars in tight skirts," she said. "You put your bottom in first and then swing your legs in together. When you're getting out, its legs out together first. It's really all about keeping your knees together. Don't worry, it will soon come naturally."

It was only a few minutes' drive to the multi-storey car park at the shopping centre, but by the time they had got there and parked, Dan was close to panic. It took all the courage he could summon to get out of the car - legs first - and his heart was thumping so hard he was surprised it could not be heard outside his body. His mother smiled at him encouragingly, took his arm again and led him to the mall entrance.

As they entered through the swing doors, Dan faltered: the place was packed with shoppers. "I can't do this," he whispered and tried to go back through the doors, but his mother held on tightly to his arm. "Yes you can" she said. "H & M is just across the way, we'll start there."

She more or less dragged him across the concourse and into H & M where he stood behind her, looking furtively this way and that, while she started riffling through the dress racks, pulling out one after another and, to his intense embarrassment, holding them up against him to see how they looked. "Please Mum," he muttered, "do you have to do this?"   "'Course I do."

"Does that mean I won't have to try anything on?" he asked hopefully.

"Don't be silly. Of course you'll have to try them on."

Dan was in a funk. "What will happen if they find out about me?" he whispered in a trembling voice.

"They won't. Now come on, we've got a lot to do. This way."

Sarah headed for the changing room with a pile of outfits over her arm. Dan followed close behind, his heart in his mouth. He was horrified at the prospect of entering a women's changing room, but more horrified at the prospect of being left alone on the shop floor.

It turned out he had little to worry about. In the privacy of a cubicle Dan discovered it was no hassle to take off his dress and try on a new one in front of a full-length mirror. A couple of times his mother left him alone to get a different size and he listened to conversations in adjoining cubicles, wondering what they would do if they knew that it was a boy next door. He liked a lot of the dresses and skirts that his mother had picked out for him and slowly began to realise that he was enjoying himself.

Three hours later they were sitting together having tea and cakes in the John Lewis restaurant on the top floor of the shopping centre surrounded by packages that more or less contained a complete new wardrobe for a teenage girl. Dan had long since stopped fretting about being unmasked; his main problems were that his training bra was a little tight and his ankle boots had given him blisters, but otherwise he was as happy as he could be.

His mother noticed that when he sat down and crossed his long legs he made no attempt to pull down the hem of his skirt and pretended to be unaware of stares from the occasional man passing by. She said nothing, but smiled inwardly. She was amazed at how quickly he had gained confidence; once he was certain he was passing as a girl successfully he took a full part in the shopping, taking a real interest, looking at things for himself and asking his mother's opinion. He only baulked at the lingerie in Victoria's Secret, whispering to his mother that it would be hard to hide his willy in a G-string made of lace. Sarah laughed.

As they went from shop to shop she was pleased to discover that Dan had good taste, rejecting dresses that were too glaring or too revealing or too short, or shoes with ridiculous heels, or flashy jewellery. She reflected, more than once, that their shopping spree was probably how it would have been if Alice was still alive; just the two of them, shopping for fun.

He needed to pee twice and insisted his mother accompany him into the Ladies. In fact he had not left her side since they had arrived at the shopping centre so she was surprised when, in the restaurant, he said he'd wait at their table while she went to the loo. "Are you sure you'll be OK?" she asked. He laughed. "Of course. I'd rather sit here than lug all our packages into the Ladies. And anyway my feet hurt." What he did not tell his mother was that he had made eye contact with two boys on the other side of the restaurant and they had both waved when he had smiled at them.

There was a queue in the Ladies and Sarah was longer than she anticipated she would be. As she re-entered the restaurant she could see, immediately, that there were two young men standing at their table talking to Dan, who seemed to be laughing. She hesitated, then stepped to one side, half hidden by a pillar, to watch. Whatever the young men were saying required a great deal of arm waving and Dan was laughing so hard he had to reach into his handbag for a tissue to dab at his eyes. One of the young men said something that made Dan blush and flutter his eyelashes as the young man punched keys in his mobile phone.

Sarah realised that not only were these two young men flirting with Dan, *but he was flirting back.* And in that moment something became blindingly obvious, something she kicked herself for not recognising much sooner. Her son was obviously gay.

She could hardly extend her absence any longer. As she approached their table, Dan said something to the young men who turned and smiled at her. She judged them to be around 18 or 19, both very good looking. "I hope you don't mind," one of them said, "but your daughter looked so lonely sitting here by herself that we thought we'd tell her a few jokes."

Sarah returned his smile. "That's fine as long as they were not too filthy; she's only 15." Dan was startled by his mother referring to him, for the first time, as "she".

"Oh no, all good clean fun," the boy said. "We'd better get going. 'Bye Daisy, see you around."

Sarah's eyebrows shot up, but Dan warned her with a pleading look and a slight shake of his head to say nothing. "'Bye," he said returning their waves as they walked out.

Sarah, too, waved and then turned to Dan. "*Daisy?*"

"I know. But they asked me what my name was. I could hardly say it was Dan could I?"

"Obviously not, but *Daisy?* Where did that come from?"

"I dunno. It was just the first name that came into my head." This wasn't quite true. While he was cross-dressing in secret he fantasised about giving himself a name that was one hundred per cent girly, that could not possibly be mistaken for a boy, that could not be diminutised, and he came up with Daisy. He began to think of his cross-dressing as Daisy time; Daisy became his alter ego.

"Well, you'd better be Daisy from now on, hadn't you?" Sarah said, "at least when you're wearing a dress. I saw one of the boys doing something with his mobile phone. What was that all about?"

Dan hesitated. "Well, he said he often visited Brighton and perhaps we could meet so I gave him my mobile number."

Sarah was faintly shocked. "Was that wise?"

"Why not?"

"Well, first of all you are only 15 years old and second you are only just starting out on this experiment with your gender. It might be a bit premature to think about dating. And if you were to meet, you would obviously have to meet him as a girl…"

"Yes, I know. Well, he probably won't call anyway, so you don't have to worry."

"Maybe, but you need to understand that if you are going to dress like a girl and behave like a girl, there are certain things you need to think about. For example, you are sitting there with your legs crossed and showing an awful lot of leg…"

Dan looked down at his legs as if he was taken aback by what his mother was saying. But the truth was that he knew that his skirt had hitched up; he knew he was showing a lot of leg in his black tights; he knew the two boys on the other side of the restaurant had had a good look; and he was *enjoying* it.

But to please his mother he pulled down the hem of his dress an inch or two.

CHAPTER 6

Toby hated what was going on, partly because he could not understand it. He did not know why his brother had gone into Alice's bedroom and got dressed up in her clothes and he did not much care; he could not imagine why any boy would want to do that, but he had always thought his older brother was a bit strange. He did not even like football and he was useless at all sport. Toby had often thought Dan looked a bit like a girl, with his long hair, and he'd heard some of the girls in the salon saying the same, but he'd never thought that he'd actually put on a dress. What a weirdo!

That Saturday when his mother and his brother had gone shopping, she had sent him a text message in the afternoon saying that they would be late getting back home. He did not think much about it, only that he was grateful she had not made him go along too and miss football. The game was in Eastbourne against a team which had usually beaten them, but this time they had won, 3-2, and Toby had scored the winning goal.

He arrived home in a state approaching ecstasy and was only disappointed his Mum was not there to share his triumph. He texted her to ask where she was and his brother replied to say they were in the car and would be home in an hour. Where R U? he asked.

Somewhere around Portsmouth was the reply.

Where have U been?

Southampton.

Y?

Surprise. U hv 2 wait till we get home.

Toby made himself a sandwich from the fridge then went upstairs to play on his computer. He was engrossed in *Outcast: Second Contact* and was startled when he heard his mother call out "Toby, we're home." He went to the top of the stairs and saw both his mother and his brother were laden with shopping bags, but he was bursting to tell her his news.

"Mum, we won 3-2 and guess who scored the winning goal? Me!"

Sarah "That's great, Toby. Well done. Now can you help Dan carry these bags up to his room and then come down because I want to talk to you?"

"What is all this stuff? Is it all for him? Why can't he bring it up?"

Sarah sighed. "Toby, I'm tired. It's been a long day. Just do as I ask. Please."

Toby stomped down the stairs, grabbed an armful of bags, carried them up and threw them into his brother's room. He paid no attention to the contents. Dan followed him up with the remaining packages then disappeared into his room.

Back downstairs Toby found his mother in the kitchen pouring herself a glass of wine. "What's going on?" he demanded.

Sarah told him to sit down and then explained that after a lot of thought she had decided to let his brother cross-dress at home, if that was what he wanted, and that they had been out on a shopping spree to get him everything he needed. There was no harm in him dressing as a girl, she said, and it was better that he should do it openly, but for the time being it was important that no one else knew. Later that might change, but at the moment he was to tell no one.

Toby listened to his mother in silence, hardly able to believe his ears. When she had finished, he did not pretend to hide his disgust. "So I've got to put up with seeing my brother poncing about in a skirt, have I? What happens when my friends come round? Am I supposed to say he's my sister, when they all know he's my brother?"

"I don't know," Sarah admitted. "We'll have to work that out. Maybe we'll have to have days when he is not allowed to cross dress so you can have your friends round. I know this is hard for you to accept, Toby, but it is very important that you try and understand. These days lots of young people like to experiment with their gender and their sexuality…"

Toby interrupted. "Dan's gay isn't he?"

Sarah avoided a direct answer. "I'm not sure whether he is or he isn't, but either way it does not matter. What matters is that we should understand and help him if he is feeling the need to dress like a girl. Maybe he'll grow out of it, maybe he won't. As I said earlier, there's nothing wrong with it…"

"You try and tell that to my friends. They have lots of nasty names for people like Dan…"

"I'm sure they have, but I don't want to hear them. When he's in a dress he thinks of himself as Daisy…"

"Daisy! Christ, I can't believe this is happening," Toby muttered. "Have I got to call him fucking Daisy…?"

"Watch your language, young man. No, you…"

At that moment the door opened and Dan walked in wearing one of his new dresses. This time Toby did not laugh. He just looked his brother up and down, very slowly, shook his head and walked out without another word.

"I wanted you to see how I looked," Dan said, "but…

"Don't worry, sweetheart," his mother said. "It's hard for him to understand, but he'll soon come round…"

* * * * *

Over the next few weeks the family worked out an arrangement that would accommodate Dan's cross-dressing. He was either to stay in his school clothes, or stay in his room, when Toby invited friends round. If someone called at the door unexpectedly he would disappear into his room. Toby needed no further prompting about not telling anyone what was going on; frankly, he was ashamed of what his brother was doing and as anxious as his mother that no one should know.

What was a surprise to Sarah was how quickly Toby's disgust turned to indifference; it soon no longer bothered him to find Dan sitting about at home in a dress or a skirt and wearing make-up. Initially, he would make a face or a sarcastic remark ("Nice dress - it would look even better on a girl") but after a very short time it seemed he more or less expected to find Dan dressed as "Daisy" (although he completely refused to use that name). But it maddened him when his mother occasionally used female pronouns for his brother or sometimes referred to him as his "sister". "He's not a fucking girl" he would mutter angrily under his breath and be reprimanded for his bad language.

For Dan it was like entering a whole new, and exciting, world. He was thrilled to open a drawer in his bedroom and find it packed with coloured tights, all neatly rolled up, knickers and bras. His wardrobe contained more dresses and skirts than trousers and shirts. Three pairs of high-heeled shoes, a pair of ankle boots also with heels, and two pairs of ballet pumps were lined up alongside his trainers. Make-up was scattered across a table top in front of a mirror. Most days, unless there was PE, he wore knickers and tights under his school trousers, despite his mother warning him he was taking a risk that someone would notice.

Even if his brother was having friends round, the temptation to put on a dress was so strong he usually changed and simply stayed in his room with the door locked, waiting for them to go and Toby to give him the all clear. He was nearly caught one afternoon when he was half way down the stairs in a mini skirt when Toby opened the front door unexpectedly and walked in with two friends. He tried not to panic and just turned round and went back to his room, but both boys had caught a glimpse of him. "Who was that?" one of them asked. Toby, thinking quickly, explained that "she" was a cousin who was staying with them for a few days.

"Why did she run back to her room?" the friend persisted.

"She's shy," Toby explained, irritated that he had to use a female pronoun for his brother.

"Pity, she's got great legs. What a looker, I bet she…"

"Yeah OK," Toby interrupted, not wanting to hear what his friend was going to say, assuming, probably correctly, it was going to be smutty. "Look, come into the kitchen. There's some Red Bull in the fridge."

He recounted the conversation to his brother later, after his friends had left, hoping to embarrass him, but Dan just laughed and blushed and seemed pleased. Toby was mystified.

What really pissed him off was the way their mother seemed to have forgotten that his brother was a boy and started treating him as if he really was a girl. She could not hide how pleased she was to come home and find Dan in a dress; she'd almost always tell him how nice he looked. They talked constantly about clothes and make-up and hair styles and other stupid girly stuff all the time and they often sat together in the evening flicking through fashion magazines or trawling fashion websites.

Toby tried to avoid looking at his brother when he was dressed as a girl, although he did puzzle over what he did with his dick when he was wearing a very tight skirt; there was never, he ascertained by furtive peeking, even a slight bulge in the front. Toby masturbated frequently and knew that after jerking off his willy almost disappeared and he wondered if his brother had to jerk off before he put on a skirt, but he dismissed the idea because if his brother's dick was anything like his it would be back to its normal size in a matter of minutes. It was a mystery that remained a mystery because he certainly wasn't going to ask.

As long as no one knew what was going on, Toby could tolerate the situation but when his mother told him that Dan was going to start going out as a girl he complained loudly and vigorously. It wasn't fair on him, he protested; Dan was sure to be seen and then the word would be out and he'd be a laughing stock, having a brother who was a cross-dresser.

"Don't you understand, Toby," his mother replied gently, "this is not about you, this is about Daisy.."

"DAISY? DAISY?" Toby shouted, "don't *you* understand that Daisy doesn't exist?" And with that he stalked off to his bedroom and slammed the door.

Actually Sarah was taken completely by surprise when, after the fuss that Dan had made about going shopping, he announced he was ready to start going out and about in a dress. Taking a cue from his brother, he asked if she could perhaps tell their nosey neighbour that a girl cousin was staying with them to explain who he was. "Are you sure about this?" she had asked. "Would you like me to come with you?"

He shook his head. "No, I'll be fine. I've decided that I can't let wearing a dress keep me a prisoner in the house. If anyone thinks they recognise me, I'll deny it and I'll explain the resemblance by saying I'm Dan's cousin."

"If you are sure…?"

"Don't worry. I'll be fine. I'll see you later."

"Wait. Where are you going?"

"Just for a walk along the seafront to get some air."

"OK. Be careful now."

"I will. 'Bye."

After he had closed the door behind him, Sarah went to the window to watch him walk down the street in the direction of the seafront. In his black mini skirt, patterned tights and ankle boots, with a bag over his shoulder and his hair in a pony tail, he looked, she was encouraged to see, just like any other pretty teenage girl. She was surprised how quickly he had learned to walk in heels.

She wondered what had brought on this change of heart, this new-found confidence to step outside in a skirt. She had no idea, but she was certainly pleased about it, pleased that her oldest son was becoming more and more relaxed about dressing as a girl.

What she did not know, because Dan had never mentioned it, was that he had been in regular daily contact, by text, with Mark Tisdale, one of the boys he had met in the restaurant at John Lewis during their shopping spree. He had been surprised and thrilled when his phone pinged the following day and a text from Mark appeared on the screen with a smiley face. *"Hi sexy, whatya doin?"*

It was the start of a long, and increasingly intimate, text conversation during which they began to get to know each other and Dan got to learn how to respond like a girl to the attentions of another boy. He nearly broke it off when Mark asked for a topless photo, but when he indignantly refused, Mark quickly backtracked and said he had only been joking. Dan was not sure he believed him, but he giggled whenever he thought of the shock he would have caused had he agreed.

They had been exchanging messages for about three weeks when Mark said he had been able to borrow a car from a friend and he was intending to drive to Brighton so that they could meet, suggesting the following Saturday. This sent Dan into a spiral of nervous apprehension. On the one hand he really did want to see Mark again, but on the other he was terrified at the prospect. It was one thing to hang about the house in make-up and a dress, it was quite another to step outside on a date.

To buy some time he told Mark that he was going to be away for a couple of weeks - it was the school summer holiday - while he thought about what to do. He really only had two choices: he either had to break up with Mark or agree to meet him. He obviously could not make excuses forever to avoid it. It was to prepare to face meeting Mark that he started taking short walks along the seafront dressed as a girl and quickly discovered that no one took any notice of him at all, apart from rude boys who always looked at his legs and chest before looking at his face. He also discovered that he liked boys ogling him; it gave him a little thrill to know they were sizing him up without any awareness of what was between his legs.

On the morning of the day he had agreed to meet Mark he was almost paralysed with nerves and his hands were shaking so much he had to make three attempts to apply his mascara before he got it right. He tried on half a dozen different outfits, checking each one in the new full-length mirror this mother had bought for his bedroom, before decided on a floral print cotton mini dress. He was glad his mother was at work, otherwise she would certainly have picked up on his stress and quizzed him about what was going on. Toby was at home, waiting for a lift to go and play football, but he took no notice of his brother's preparations

Mark had offered to pick him up at his house, but he had refused without feeling the need to explain that his mother knew nothing about their date. They agreed to meet at the Yellow Wave Cafe on the seafront, half way between the pier and the marina, and only a short walk from the Walters' house.

Mark was already there, sitting at an outside table with a beer, when Dan arrived, his heart in his mouth. To his surprise, Mark leapt to his feet, grabbed him in a bear hug and kissed him full on the mouth. Dan's instinct was to recoil, but Mark quickly released him, grinned and said "I've been thinking of doing that for weeks. Great to see you. You look fab."

Dan blushed. He did not know what to say. No one had ever kissed him like that before. Mark drew a chair out for him and he sat down, remembering to tuck his skirt under him as he did so and to keep his knees together. He was asked what he wanted to drink and he said a flat white and while Mark went off to get it, Dan took a pair of big sunglasses out of his handbag, put them on and looked around. He reckoned that with the sunglasses covering almost a third of his face, no one would be able to recognise him; but there was no one about that he knew anyway and he began to relax.

Mark was funny and personable and Dan was soon laughing a lot, really enjoying himself. When they left to walk to the pier, Mark took his hand, intertwining his fingers with Dan's and Dan found himself blushing again, happy to be holding hands with this nice boy, who was tall and good looking and fun to be with. It was almost possible for him to believe he was the girl Mark thought he was except for the throbbing penis tucked between his legs.

On the pier they played the slots, rode the bumper cars and the roller coaster and Mark won a teddy bear on the shooting gallery which he presented to Dan with great ceremony. As they walked back along the pier, hand in hand again, Mark suggested taking a drive up onto the Downs. Dan hesitated; he needed to be home before his mother got back from the salon at around 6 o'clock. It was then half-past three; there was enough time for a drive. "OK," he said, "but I need to be back in Brighton before six."

It was not a car that Mark had borrowed, but an old, dilapidated van that wheezed and rattled as they headed up the winding road towards Ditchling and the ridge of the Downs. At the top, Mark pulled off the road, bumped along a farm track and parked on the edge of a field with a fine view across the Downs towards the sea.

"Wanna smoke?"

Dan shook his head.

"Do you mind if I do?"

Dan shook his head again.

Mark felt in the glove pocket, pulled out a pouch and began rolling a spliff with dexterous fingers. He lit up, inhaled deeply and sighed. "This," he said, blowing out a stream of acrid smoke, "is the best stuff I have ever found. Here, have a go."

He passed the spliff to Dan who took it gingerly and put it to his lips. He had had the occasional toke at parties and didn't really like it, but he took a small puff and then started coughing as he handed it back, making Mark laugh. They sat in silence, staring out through the windscreen at the view, while Mark finished his smoke, but then he immediately rolled another and lit up again.

Dan was beginning to get anxious. The single puff of marijuana had made his head swim and he felt sick. "Mark," he said, "I think we should think about heading back."

"Yeah, yeah, just let me finish this. Oh man, this is wonderful shit. The best ever. What could be nicer than sitting up here, admiring the view and getting high with a hot chick by your side?"

He pinched out his spliff and put the butt into the pouch, then leaned back his seat and stretched out to put an arm round Dan to pull him closer. Dan guessed what was coming and felt his heart quicken. He did not initially resist as Mark brushed his lips against Dan's but he then pushed his tongue deep into Dan's throat and thrust a hand up his skirt. Almost gagging, Dan pulled back and pushed Mark's hand away.

"I think we should go," he gasped, pulling down the hem of his dress.

"Oh, it's little Miss Prissy now, is it?" Mark sneered, suddenly angry.

"Please, Mark. Please. Can we go?"

"Sure, just as soon as you deal with this…"

To Dan's horror, Mark unzipped his jeans and pulled out his prick - a big, ugly thing, Dan thought, as stiff as a ramrod. "You know what to do, don't you?" Mark demanded, holding the base of his prick with one hand and wagging it at Dan. The smell of it filled the van and made Dan even more nauseous.

Dan shook his head. "I'm not doing that," he whispered. "Please, I don't like this. Please, let's go."

"I've told you. We'll go just as soon as you get me off. And when I come I want you to swallow it. Do you understand? No spitting out."

Dan, close to tears, could not understand why Mark was so angry. "Please, Mark…"

"Don't tell me you haven't blown guys before. Do you know what my mate said when we first saw you in that restaurant? You were sitting just across the way, giving us the eye and flashing your legs. Don't you remember? My mate said 'There's a girl who's gagging for it if ever there was one'."

Dan began to cry. "I just want to go home…" he sobbed.

To his relief, Mark began to squirm in his seat and although Dan did not dare look, he thought he was putting his prick away.

"Well, if you're not going to give me a BJ," he grunted, "you're going to give me a fuck. Get in the back."

Mark grabbed Dan's arm as if to pull him into the back of the van but Dan, now thoroughly frightened, shook himself free, opened the van door and jumped out. He hesitated for a second, not knowing which way to go, giving Mark time to get out himself and run round to where he was standing.

Dan turned and tried to run away, but Mark was on him before he taken more than a few paces. Mark knocked him to the ground and then fell on top of him, using his weight to pin him down. Dan struggled, but in vain; Mark was bigger and stronger. He started shouting for help, but Mark put a hand over his mouth. Dan could feel Mark's other hand tugging at the waistband of his tights. He tried to tell him to stop but could only make strangulated noises behind the hand covering his mouth.

He heard his dress rip as Mark finally pulled down his tights and knickers and exposed his genitalia. They both instantly stopped fighting. Mark stared, unable to believe his eyes. "Fucking hell," he murmured.

Dan, lying quite still, paralysed with fear, tried to cover himself up. "I'm sorry," he whimpered, "I should have told you…"

"Yes, you fucking should have," Mark shouted, getting to his feet. "You're a fucking freak. I don't date fucking freaks."

Dan pulled up his knickers and tights as best he could, then stood up and smoothed the skirt of his dress. Before he could say a word Mark hit him, full in the face, with a clenched fist and knocked him down again. Blood gushed from Dan's nose onto his dress.

Mark looked down on him without pity. "Fucking freak," he shouted again and kicked Dan in the crutch as hard as he could. Dan howled in pain.

Mark shut the open passenger door of the van with a kick, walked around to the driver's side, got in, slammed the door and gunned the engine. Dan, still lying on the ground, was terrified that he was going to run him over and tried to crawl towards a fence, but Mark just reversed and tore off, bouncing back along the rutted track towards the main road.

Dan never knew pain like it. His head was ringing and it felt as if his genitals were on fire: He gritted his teeth and pulled himself into a sitting position so he could lean with his back against the fence, then searched in his handbag for his phone. He punched a number with trembling fingers and held it to his ear.

"Mum, I need help."

"Oh my God, Dan, what's happened?"

"I'll tell you later. What I need right now is for you to pick me up."

"Are you OK?"

"No, I've been beaten up."

"Oh my God, shall I call the police?"

"No, Mum, please don't do that. Just come and get me."

"Where are you?"

"That's the thing. I don't really know. I'm up on the Downs somewhere…"

CHAPTER 7

It took Sarah more than an hour to find Dan, even though she had told him to leave his phone switched on to use as a beacon. When she finally arrived, she found him still sitting on the ground and leaning against the fence, with his dress torn from one shoulder, holes in his tights and blood caked under his nose and on the bodice of his dress.

    He began to cry again as his mother stepped out of her car and ran towards him. She knelt at his side, put her arms round him and drew him to her. "Never mind, never mind," she said, stroking his back. "I'm here now. Mummy's got you. Never mind."

She helped him to his feet and into the front passenger seat of her car. When she was settled into the driver's seat alongside him she asked if she needed to take him to hospital. He shook his head. "I, I don't think so, Mum," he said between sobs. "I don't think anything is broken and the pain is getting less all the time."

"OK," she said. "Dry your eyes. You'd better try and tell me what happened."

Dan told her everything. How he had been secretly exchanging text messages with one of the boys he had met in John Lewis, how they had arranged to meet, how nice he was at first, how he had made him laugh, how he had made him really feel like a girl, how he had no worries when Mark suggested driving up into the Downs and the how everything had gone wrong after he started smoking a joint, how he got angry when he refused to give him a blow job, how he tried to drag him into the back of the van, how he jumped out and tried to run away, then how he had been knocked down and, and… he shook his head and fell silent.

"You've got to try and tell me everything," his mother said gently, "I know it's hard, but I have to know."

Dan took a deep breath. "He held me down on the ground and pulled down my tights and my knickers and saw I was a boy…." Dan started crying again. It took him a little while to get control of himself before he continued. "… Then he got really, really mad, started swearing at me and calling me a freak and other horrible things and when I got up he hit me in the face and knocked me down and then kicked me… kicked me down there. It really, really hurt. Then he got into his van and I thought he was going run me over… I really did, Mum, he was so mad… I tried to get out of his way but he just drove off. That's it. That's what happened."

Sarah swallowed hard, trying to contain her fury. Dan was wrong to deceive her, of course he was, but he was only a kid confused about his gender and did not deserve to be attacked because he was wearing a dress. This Mark bastard was a potential rapist and needed to be stopped…

Dan interrupted her swirling thoughts. "Maybe I should have told him, Mum, but I was frightened he would dump me. He obviously thought I was a girl and we got on really well. I think he liked me and I liked him and I thought we could maybe go out together for a bit as boy friend and girl friend…"

His mother shrugged. "Maybe, sweetheart, I don't know. But you were taking a big risk, you must see that. Sooner or later he was going to find out about you and I think the longer he had been with you, not knowing about you, the angrier he might have been. We need to talk about this another time. The first thing we have to do now is to make sure this bastard gets punished for what he has done. I think we should drive straight to Brighton police station and tell them…"

Dan gulped and drew in his breath. "No, Mum, we can't do that. Don't you see? I can't tell anyone what has happened, ever. They're going to blame me for pretending to be a girl and conning him, they're going to say it is my fault for leading him on, agreeing to go on a drive with him up into the Downs, what did I expect? I won't get any sympathy from the police, you know that."

Sarah thought it over and realised Dan was probably right. Even if he agreed to give evidence against his attacker, it would be a wretched ordeal for him. She sighed. "Let's go home and get you cleaned up," she said.

* * * *

When Dan got home, he went up to his room, took off all his clothes and threw them into a corner, intending they should be dumped in the garbage; he never wanted to wear any of them ever again. He had a long shower, the hot water easing the lingering pain in his genitals, and went straight to bed.

Next morning - it was a Sunday with no visitors - he would normally have put on a dress, or a skirt and top. Instead, he slipped into an old pair of his jeans and a T-shirt and went downstairs.

His mother raised her eyebrows when he walked into the kitchen. "What's this?" she said.

Dan slumped into a chair at the table, twisted a hank of his hair with one hand and shrugged. "Nothing," he said, meaninglessly. "Just that I'm done with Daisy, that's all."

This was the last thing Sarah expected. "What do you mean, you're done with Daisy?"

"Just that I'm not dressing as a girl any more."

"Why, sweetheart?"

"I just don't want to do it any more."

Sarah could see the girl she longed to have around suddenly slipping away and was desperate to salvage the situation. "This is because of what happened yesterday, isn't it?"

Dan hesitated, then nodded.

"Don't you see that if you abandon Daisy now that bastard who attacked you will have won? Do you want that? Do you want to allow him to stop you doing something you like doing and which hurts no one?"

"No of course not, Mum, but I've been thinking… What's the point of me dressing as a girl? I'll never be a girl. I'll always be a boy pretending to be a girl and in the end I'll always get found out…"

Dan was close to tears again. Sarah pulled up a chair to sit beside him and put her arm round him.

"Look sweetheart, I'm not going to force you to do anything you don't want to do, but you have to understand that the world is a very different place now from when I was your age. Gender is not fixed any more, it's fluid. It's perfectly OK for boys to dress as girls and girls to dress as boys, if they want to. Everyone knows and understands that these days. You were just unlucky yesterday to come across some bigoted neanderthal whose masculinity was threatened when he discovered you were not a girl. But you did nothing wrong, you must understand that. You do, don't you?"

Dan nodded, uncertainly.

"If you don't want to be Daisy any more, that's obviously your right, your decision. No one is going to force you. But I, for one, will be sad. I've really loved having Daisy around these past few months and I thought you were enjoying it, too."

"Yes, I was, but… Oh, I don't know…" Dan started to cry.

Sarah took a tissue from the pocket of her apron and dried his eyes. "Don't cry, sweetheart, please don't cry. There's really nothing to cry about…"

While she was comforting him, she decided the moment was right for her to introduce something she had been thinking about for some time. She recognised it was a do-or-die attempt to save Daisy and she thought through what she was going to say very carefully before opening her mouth. "You know what I think has been causing you extra stress," she said slowly.

Dan, a picture of misery, shook his head.

"I think keeping everything secret has put an extra strain on you and there is really no need for it. If you were to decide you want to keep on dressing as Daisy, there is absolutely no reason in the world why you have to keep it secret and skulk around at home hoping no one will see you. Why should you? You are not doing anything wrong, are you? You are not doing anything to be ashamed of. Why…"

Dan interrupted her impatiently. "What about Toby? What about everyone at school? What about all the family? What about my friends? I won't have any friends if everyone knows about me dressing as a girl."

Sarah was silent for a moment, then she delivered the *coup de grâce* to his argument. "Supposing," she said, "you began living as Daisy all the time? Obviously it would take everyone a little time to get used to it, but I think you would be surprised how quickly everyone would accept it."

"You mean go to school as a girl, live as a girl 24/7?"

"Absolutely."

Dan's eyes widened. It had never occurred to him that there was such a possibility. His mother watched him carefully as he began considering what she had said.

Even without make-up he looked as much like a girl as he did a boy, particularly with his long blond hair. She tried to fathom from his expression what he was thinking without success. It was obviously a huge decision for him to make and she did not want to rush him, so she sat quietly waiting for him to speak.

Eventually he shook his head. "I wish I could do it, but I can't. I'm not brave enough. I would get torn apart at school if I showed up wearing a skirt."

"Doesn't your school have trouser uniforms and skirt uniforms? I remember when they introduced it they made a big thing about pupils being able to wear the uniform of the gender they most closely identified with."

"Yeah, but it was just old Donkey Drop wanting to show how trendy he is." ("Donkey Drop" was the nickname all the students used for the headmaster, James Horsfall.)

"Still, you could if you wanted."

Dan shook his head again. "What about Dad? He would go mad if he found out I was living as a girl."

Sarah snorted. "I don't think you need worry about your father. He's made it clear he's not the slightest bit interested in us." In reality, Sarah got a little frisson of pleasure whenever she thought of the fury with which her former husband would react to the news.

"What about the family and all my cousins?" Dan continued. "What about when we all get together at Christmas? They'd fall about laughing if I arrived at Auntie Eve's wearing a dress."

"Dan, I'm not pretending it would be easy. All I am saying is that it is a possibility, something you might think worth considering. You know you can pass as a girl, you know you enjoy dressing as a girl. There is not a reason in the world why you couldn't live as a girl, if you decided that was what you wanted to do. That's all I'm saying. Obviously it would be an upheaval, but if you decided to do it I honestly think you would be very surprised how quickly everyone accepted the situation, accepted you as a girl."

She could see he was thinking carefully about what she had said. While he had raised objections, he had not categorically dismissed what she had suggested. She decided to say no more and let him mull over their conversation.

For his part, Dan was in turmoil. His mother had thrown another grenade into his lap, just as she had when she announced she was going to take him shopping for dresses. Until that minute he had not in his wildest dreams considered the possibility of what she was proposing. It was so awesome, so off the wall, so amazing that it had never entered his consciousness. He was still far from convinced that it could ever happen, but the more he thought about it the more he wondered … could it? Could he go to school as a girl? Could he wear a dress when all the family gathered, as usual at Aunt Eve's house, for Christmas? Could he live, full time, as a girl?

He and his mother ate breakfast together in silence, both preoccupied with their own thoughts. Toby had already gone out to meet his friends. Dan shook his head when his mother asked him if he would like another slice of toast. He finished his orange juice and made to leave the kitchen and when his mother asked him where he was going he said, with studied casualness, "Oh, I think I'll just go and put on a dress."

After he had left, his mother felt she could have danced around the room.

CHAPTER 8

A week passed and neither Dan nor his mother mentioned their conversation at the breakfast table the previous Sunday. Sarah didn't want Dan to feel he was being pushed into making a decision and was encouraged that there was no more talk of him being "done with Daisy"; he was continuing to dress as a girl after school.

While Dan said nothing, the subject was constantly on his mind. At the stop waiting for the school bus, he imagined standing there in the girls' uniform - a white blouse, black and white check pleated skirt and black tights. He tried to anticipate the reaction of his friends. He wondered what the family would think. He had a couple of old fogey uncles who he was sure would be outraged if he started living as a girl. Toby would be pretty pissed off, too, but he wasn't worried about that.

He spent a lot of time trawling the internet for more information, for stories about gay boys living as girls. Any doubts he had had about his sexual orientation had been swept away by Mark's initial kiss and by his (Dan's) excitement when they walked along the pier hand in hand. He was reassured to find plenty of boys just like him; he was not alone. And he was greatly cheered to realise that he was a lot prettier than many of them. Some could not disguise for a moment that they were male and he wondered what was the point of trying to pretend they were girls when everyone could see they were boys.

He assumed they were probably all gay, like him. He knew that if he came out to his mother she would be sympathetic. Perhaps, he thought, that was the simplest solution. But for Dan it was not just the fact that he was gay that occupied his thoughts; it was his overwhelming desire to dress as a girl. He had not changed his mind about the future - he still had no desire to undergo sexual reassignment surgery - he just wanted to *live* as a girl, not *be* one. In this way he could keep his options open and always return to living as a boy, if that was what he wanted in the end. It would be the best of both worlds, he thought.

He waited until the weekend before he told his mother. "I've been thinking about what you said and I think I would like to give it a shot."

"Oh really, dear," Sarah replied, pretending incomprehension to hide her elation. "What would you like to give a shot?" She wanted him to say it out loud so there could be no equivocation.

Dan hesitated. "You know, living as a girl."

"Are you sure?"

Another hesitation. "I think so."

Sarah, smiling broadly, got up from the table and walked round to give her son a hug. "I think that would be absolutely lovely. As I said last week it's not going to be easy, but you know I'll help you all the way. Have you thought about how we should go about it?"

Dan shrugged and shook his head. Fortunately, his mother had. In fact she had thought of little else for the past week.

"OK, I think we will have to plan it bit by bit. First we have to warn Toby what is going to happen, then family and friends will have to know and finally we'll need the school to approve you attending as a girl. I think you should leave Toby and the family to me and then we'll deal with the school together. Does that make sense?"

Dan nodded uncertainly. He had expected his mother to take over but he wasn't sure he wanted it to happen so quickly and was already beginning to get cold feet. "Maybe we should wait a little…"

Sarah sighed. "Honestly sweetie, the sooner we start this thing off the sooner you'll be over the hardest bits and the sooner you can start living 24/7 as a girl. That's what you want isn't it?"

Another hesitant nod.

"OK, now stop fretting and leave everything to me. I'll talk to Toby as soon as he gets back from football and then I'll talk to Auntie Eve when I have coffee with her tomorrow morning."

* * * * *

As Sarah had expected, Toby was sullenly resigned when, later that day, she broke the news to him that his brother Dan was to become Daisy.

"What do you mean?"

"I mean that very soon Dan will be living as a girl."

"You mean the whole time?"

"Yes."

"What about school?"

"What about it?"

"Is he going to go to school in the girls' uniform?"

"Yes, of course."

Toby grimaced. "That's *so* stupid!" he shouted.

"Don't shout at me Toby. And no, it's not the least bit stupid."

"So what am I supposed to tell my friends?"

"You'll tell them that from now on your brother has chosen to live as a girl."

"So everyone will know that my so-called brother is going to be pouncing about in a skirt pretending he's a girl, is that it? Oh, great. That's just great…"

Sarah did her best to keep her temper. "Toby, can't you be a little bit more understanding? This has not been an easy decision for him to make and he's going to need all the love and support we can give him."

"*Understanding*?" Toby sneered. "No, I can't be understanding because I don't *understand*. I don't understand anything any more and I certainly don't understand why you are letting Dan do this and making our family look… look…"

He struggled for the right word, could not find it and stormed out of the room, slamming the door as he left.

Sarah sighed. This wasn't going to be easy; she had known that from the start.

* * * * *

"You cannot be serious!" Eve shrieked, so loudly that three or four people nearby turned to stare at her. She smiled at them, waved a hand as if to apologise and whispered to her sister "I'm sorry. It was just… well, a bit of a surprise… To say the least."

The sisters were sitting at their usual table in the back of Small Batch Coffee Roasters, a cafe in Jubilee Street not far from Sarah's salon, where they met every

Monday morning to gossip and laugh and bond. Although they were completely different in character, they looked similar and were very close, best friends as well as sisters, with no secrets from each other. Eve, the older, was the capable, sensible one, happily married to a man she had met at university and a full-time mother to three strapping well-mannered boys who, everyone agreed, were a credit to her. Eve's husband, Charlie Evans, was an architect and keen sailor; the family spent most summer holidays on their boat, an old gaff cutter, in Cornwall. Sarah had always been flighty, a difficult teenager who lost her virginity at the age of 14 and then went through one boy-friend after another, breaking hearts along the way until she eventually married Tristram.

When Sarah's marriage broke up it was Eve who helped her sort everything out and when Alice was killed in that terrible accident, it was Eve to whom Sarah turned for solace and support.

Eve could see her sister was nervous the moment she arrived at Small Batch. Sarah was already there - which was unusual, she was habitually late - with a latte in front of her and a look on her face that Eve knew well. It was a look that said please help, or please understand, or please make something bad go away.

"What's up?" she said as she sat down.

Sarah managed a wan smile. "I've got something to tell you and I don't know where to begin."

"Try the beginning."

Sarah took a deep breath and then launched into her story, how she had found Dan wearing Alice's clothes, how upset she was, how she did not know what to do and how she finally decided that it would be better for him to cross-dress openly, if that was what he wanted to do, and how she had taken him shopping in Southampton.

"Why Southampton?"

"Well it was far enough away for him not to run into anyone he knew."

"Why should that matter?"

Sarah let out a little grunt of frustration. "Eve, you don't get it, do you? I was taking Dan out shopping for girls' clothes, so he had to be dressed as a girl. That's why he didn't want to be seen by anyone he knew."

Eve gasped. "You took Dan out shopping in a *dress?* Sarah, are you mad?"

"No. It was fun actually. Dan really enjoyed it."

"What, he went into women's changing rooms to try stuff on and all that?"

Sarah nodded.

"Christ, I can't believe this. Have you any idea of what you are doing, Sarah? I've always thought Dan was a little bit effeminate but I never imagined he would want to start wearing dresses. Is he gay, do you think?"

Sarah nodded again. "Yes, I'm certain he is gay, but I think he is attracted to boys the way a girl is attracted to boys, if that makes any sense."

"No, it doesn't. Not to me."

"Don't you understand, Eve, that gender today does not mean what it did when we were growing up? Young people today often think of gender as a choice, rather than a birthright. The fact is that Dan is choosing to identify as a girl and I have to understand that as his mother and do everything I can to help him."

"So what does that mean?"

"It means that very shortly Dan will start living, full time, as a girl."

It was at that point that Eve could not stop herself bursting out "You cannot be serious!"

But Sarah made it quite clear that she was all too serious, that it was going to happen, and that she expected support from all the family, her sister in particular. They talked for a long time and in the end Eve accepted that she had to go along with what was happening. They agreed it would be a good idea for Sarah to visit Eve and her family the following Sunday, with Dan in his new gender. Eve said she would explain to her boys what was going on and she promised that they would "behave".

"By the way," Eve said, "I suppose he won't want to answer to Dan when he's wearing a dress. What do we call him?"

Sarah hesitated. "Daisy," she said.

Eve laughed. *"Daisy?* Bloody hell."

Later that night Eve recounted her conversation with her sister to her husband, Charlie. At first he was convinced it was some kind of joke, but when Eve insisted that her sister had been deadly serious, he became quiet and thoughtful.

"You know what's happening here, don't you?" he asked after a moment.

Eve shook her head.

"I think Sarah is trying to resurrect Alice."

* * * * *

Sarah went straight to the salon after meeting her sister and found a package waiting for her on her desk in the back office. She recognised the label immediately - a pharmaceutical company in Belgium she had found after a lot of research on the web. Tearing the package open with trembling fingers, she took out three small brown glass bottles and a list of instructions, which she read with care. The three bottles contained low-dosage ingestible hormones - estradiol, spironolactone and spironolactone. The first would raise oestrogen levels, the second would lower testosterone and the third would support the growth of breast tissue. She checked the possible side effects: nothing too dramatic.

She had debated with herself whether to tell Dan what she was doing and decided against it; she would say they were vitamins which would keep up his spirits and his energy levels while he was going through the stress of being accepted as a girl. She felt no guilt about deceiving him; all she wanted to do was help him. That was all she had ever wanted to do, she told herself. And hormones that would boost his femininity would surely help during his transition.

Wouldn't they?

CHAPTER 9

Both Dan and Toby protested when, that evening, their mother announced that she had arranged for them all to visit their cousins at the weekend and she had promised her sister that Dan would be in a dress. "Auntie Eve's longing to meet Daisy," she explained, lamely.

Toby was the first to object. "I'm not going anywhere with that *thing*..." he shouted, pointing at his brother, "dressed as a girl. No way. Never. I'm not doing it. I'll stay home. I don't care what you say I'm..."

His mother angrily interrupted him. "Toby, stop shouting. Firstly, you'll do as you're told and secondly the quicker you get used to your brother being your sister the easier it is going to be for everyone. Now, Daisy, what do you think?"

Dan started. He was still trying to get used to his mother calling him Daisy, even though he was wearing make-up, a skirt and top. She had warned him that some day he would have to face the world as a girl, starting with the family, but he was just not ready. "Why did you have too tell Auntie Eve, so soon?" he whined. "I know I have got to come out sooner or later, but *this weekend?*"

Dan wasn't worried about showing himself to his Auntie Eve, or even his Uncle Charlie - he knew they would be kind and sympathetic. It was his cousins he was worried about - three noisy, boisterous, sports-mad boys who would just not understand and who he was sure would scream with laughter if he showed up at their house in a dress. "I can't do it, Mum," he said. "I just can't."

"Good," Toby muttered under his breath.

Sarah ignored her younger son and concentrated on his brother. "You've got to get it over with at some time, sweetheart," she said, "and the sooner the better. The longer you put it off the more difficult it is going to be, I promise you. Auntie Eve will talk to the boys, explain everything to them and extract a promise from all four that they will behave, treat you with respect and do nothing to humiliate you or make you feel embarrassed. You have got to remember you have done nothing wrong and you are doing nothing wrong. It is your right to live as you choose. Never forget that."

Dan nodded doubtfully. He cheered up slightly when his mother offered to book him a make-over at the salon on Saturday morning. "Do the girls know about me, then?" he asked his mother. In the family the staff at Sarah's salon were always known as "the girls", even though one was nearly 50.

Sarah shook her head. "No. I thought I'd tell them tomorrow. But I know they'll be thrilled. I'll get Alison to do your make-over."

Alison was the senior stylist and someone who Dan really liked. He had often, after school, watched her working with clients and dreamed, one day, of sitting in the chair having her work on him. Alison had once told him, thrillingly, that she could make him as pretty at Taylor Swift and he had never forgotten that, although he was never quite sure if she was joking.

Nevertheless, Dan still did not like being rushed by his mother. That night, lying in bed with everything churning over in his brain, he could see that what she was saying made sense, but at the same time she was not the one who was going to have to turn up at Auntie Eve's and face his cousins wearing a dress. One part of him was excited - he wanted to go out into the world as a girl - the other part was terrified. When he finally fell asleep he had troubled dreams: he was wearing a dress that had turned transparent and he realised he had forgotten to put on knickers and his cousins were lined up in front of him, laughing and pointing at his willy, clearly visible through his dress. He woke to find his nightdress soaked in sweat.

    At breakfast next morning he found his mother had put three small pills in a saucer next to this glass of orange juice on the kitchen table. When he asked what they were, and if they were for him, she explained that they were vitamins, that she was worried he was looking a little peaky, and that she wanted him to take them every day for a little while. She understood that he was obviously under a lot of stress and the pills would help. He shrugged and swallowed them with his orange juice in a single gulp.

    Toby was still grumbling, insisting he would not go anywhere with his brother dressed as a girl and he did not care what his mother said he was not going to do it. Sarah ignored him for a bit but finally lost her temper. "Toby, just shut up, will you?," she shouted. "Just shut up! I'm sick of the sound of your whining. This is nothing to do with you. Just get that into your thick head. Dan is going to become Daisy and there is nothing you can do about it. If I hear any more whining from you, I'll make you wear a dress, too. Do you understand?"

Toby went pale. "You can't do that," he muttered without much conviction. "And anyway I wouldn't do it."

"You'd be surprised what I can do," his mother replied darkly. She was gratified that he remained silent for the remainder of the breakfast and left the kitchen without another word. She did not think for a moment that she could force him to wear a dress, but if the threat was sufficient to shut him up she was satisfied.

During a coffee break at the salon, Sarah got the girls together and gave them the news that her son Dan was to become her daughter Daisy. As she predicted their reaction was positive - "awesome" was the word most used. None of them seemed particularly surprised, but then Brighton was a city where transexuals, transvestites and cross-dressers felt uniquely at home and many of them were clients at Sarah's salon. She asked Alison if she could fit Dan in on Saturday morning for a make-over and Alison said she could. "I always thought he was too pretty to be a boy," she said.

Afterwards Sarah drove to Dan's school to keep an appointment she had made secretly with the headmaster, Mr Horsfall. He was entirely sympathetic as she explained how Dan had been suffering from gender dysphoria for some time and was now identifying strongly as female and wanted to attend school as a girl. Horsfall had been one of the first headmasters in the country to announce that his school was adopting a gender neutral policy regarding uniforms - anyone could choose to wear either a skirt uniform or a trousers uniform - and he had been delighted by the attention his initiative had received in the media. He kept a recording of his interview with Good Morning Britain on ITV in his desk drawer and looked at it frequently.

Sarah was surprised and heartened when Horsfall told her that there were already a number of students taking advantage of the new rules and that there were adequate procedures in place to ensure they were not bullied or harassed in any way.

"Are they boys or girls?" Sarah could not stop herself from asking.

Horsfall shook his head. "I am afraid I am not at liberty to reveal that," he replied pompously. "The school maintains strict confidentiality for all pupils as I am sure you can understand."

Actually Horsfall was lying. No pupils had so far asked to attend school in a different gender, but he did not want to admit it as he had been invited back to the Good Morning Britain studios in six months to report on how the experiment was working out. Now he had a real candidate he was anxious to make it happen so he would have something to talk about.

"All we will need, Mrs Walter," he continued, "is a letter signed by both parents confirming your request for Dan to attend school in a skirt uniform and we will take care of the rest. When do you want it to start?"

"As soon as possible," Sarah replied, neglecting to mention that she had not even discussed it with her son, let alone his father.

"In that case, I would suggest that Dan should take the day off from school on Monday next to allow for an announcement to be made and then he can return on Tuesday in the skirt uniform. I will assign two senior girls to act as mentors while he becomes accustomed to life at school as a girl and everyone becomes accustomed to his new identity."

Sarah left the headmaster's office with a spring in her step. She said nothing about her visit to Dan, reasoning that he had enough to worry about. She justified what she was doing because she knew that there would be no question of her son attempting to pass as a boy by the time Alison had finished with him at the salon, particularly as much beauty treatment was not immediately reversible. Once an eyebrow had been plucked, it stays plucked for a long time.

The following day she delivered the required letter to the headmaster's office, having forged her former husband's signature, along with her own, at the bottom of the page.

As the week progressed, Dan got quieter and quieter at home. Sarah knew what was happening: he was getting cold feet, but she resolved to say nothing.

On Friday evening she reminded him that his appointment with Alison at the salon was for 10 o'clock the following morning and that he would obviously need to turn up dressed as Daisy.

Dan nodded glumly. Sarah sighed. "Cheer up, sweetheart," she said. "You're going for a beauty make-over, not an ordeal. Most girls would be looking forward to it."

"Yes, but I'm not a girl, am I?" he snapped.

Sarah sighed again, more heavily this time. "You've got to try and stop thinking like that. This is a new age. If you want to be a girl, you're a girl. End of. It's what is in your head, not what's between your legs, that matters. All right? I know this is hard for you but I am doing everything I can, everything in my power, to make it easier. You do know that, don't you?"

Dan nodded again and gave his mother a half-hearted smile. "That's better" she said.

He barely slept a wink that night, tossing and turning in his bed, fretting about the coming weekend, not so much about his visit to the salon, which he was secretly looking forward to, but the visit on Sunday to his cousins. His mother kept trying to reassure him that his Auntie Eve had spoken to her boys and she had assured her that they all completely understood and were expecting him to be in a dress, but he still, could not believe it.

When he finally got to sleep he had more troubled dreams, usually involving his clothes falling off in public places and hordes of people jeering and pointing at him and shrieking "See, he's not a girl, he's a boy…"

At breakfast in his nightdress, still sleepy, he was morose and uncommunicative, but his mother said nothing and did not try to cheer him up. Toby had already left the house, picked up by the father of a friend for an away match in Tunbridge Wells.

When Dan had finished his breakfast, his mother gingerly broached the subject of the day ahead. "What are you going to wear today, sweetheart?" she asked.

Dan shrugged.

"I think a simple skirt and top would be best. I wouldn't bother with tights because you'll be having your legs waxed," Sarah continued.

Dan frowned. "Why am I having my legs waxed?"

"Oh, it's just a standard part of a beauty makeover. Of course, you don't have to have it done if you don't want to. You don't have to have anything you don't want, obviously."

"OK," Dan replied. "I'd better go and get ready."

Sarah tried not to breathe a sigh of relief as Dan stood up from the table, put his cup, bowl and plate into the dishwasher and left the kitchen without another word. She was half expecting him to throw a wobbly and refuse to leave the house, and she was surprised that he was not raising some objection to her plans.

Half an hour later he came down freshly showered, wearing a polka dot mini skirt and a plain white T-shirt, minimal make-up and with his hair tied up in a pony tail. He looked gorgeous, his mother thought. She was gratified to see he was not wearing tights.

"OK," she said brightly. "Shall we go?"

* * * * *

Dan was much less nervous about leaving the house dressed as a girl than he had been at the start, but he still experienced a frisson of anxiety as he stepped out of the front door with his mother and was grateful to be able to hide behind the big sunglasses that made it virtually impossible for him to be recognised. In the event, no one was around, so there was no need for him to worry.

It was only a ten-minute drive to the salon, where Dan was greeted by all the girls as "Daisy" with great excitement. "You look so much better as a girl," one of them said to general agreement and they all laughed when Dan blushed.

Alison quickly took charge. "You know I once said you could be as pretty as Taylor Swift," she told him. Dan nodded. "Well I was wrong. When I have finished with you, you are going to be *prettier*. Will you trust me and put yourself in my hands?" Dan nodded again and smiled, secretly thrilled, while his mother stood behind him, listening intently. Alison caught her eye, raised an eyebrow and Sarah gently inclined her head. They had discussed, the previous day, what they had planned for him.

The next three hours passed in a whirl. Dan had little idea what was going on, other than that it required Alison's total concentration and his complete cooperation. She swivelled his chair away from the mirror so he could not see what she was doing. He yelped when she began threading his eyebrows but only raised an objection when she announced she was going to pierce his ears. "Won't it hurt?" he asked. "Don't be silly," she replied, "you won't feel a thing." And he didn't: just a numbing cold in his ear lobes and a click.

"OK Daisy," Alison said at last, "do you want to take a look at yourself?"

"Please," he replied.

She turned his chair to face the mirror and Dan had a moment of pure disorientation when, for a second, he simply did not recognise himself. Then he gasped. "Oh my God," he said. "Is that me?"

Alison laughed. "See, I told you I'd make your prettier than Taylor Swift."

"Oh my God," he said again. "I'm a girl."

It was true. Alison had removed every vestige of his masculinity. His hair, cut and styled in a bob with a deep fringe, was highlighted in blue and pink and curled. His eyebrows were shaped into thin black arches and his eyelashes were thicker, longer and blacker. His lips were plumper, and redder. In each of his earlobes was a gold sleeper stud.

He stared at himself with disbelief and then, inexplicably to Alison, he began to cry.

Alison was horrified. "What's the matter, kiddo," she asked. "It's what you wanted isn't it?"

"I suppose so," he sobbed, "but… but… how am I going to go school like this?"

Alison was shocked. "Hasn't your mother told you?" she asked.

"Told me what?"

"Wait there. I'd better go and get her."

Alison hurried into the back office where Sarah was going through the accounts. "Daisy's done," she said, "but she's rather upset and worried about going to school. You told me that from next week she'd be going as a girl. Didn't you tell her?"

Sarah had the grace to look faintly shame-faced. "No," she said' "I thought I'd wait until today when she could see the result of the make-over. Leave it to me."

Sarah got up from her desk and swept into the salon where Dan was still staring at his reflection in the mirror and dabbing his eyes with a tissue to prevent his mascara from running. Alison had done an even better job than she had hoped. Her son, she realised with a thrill, would never be mistaken for a boy the way he looked now. "Sweetheart, you look fabulous. Alison has worked wonders. But why are you crying? I thought you'd be pleased."

Dan shook his head. "Don't you see, Mum, I can't got to school like this. I mean I look like a girl…"

"That's what you wanted wasn't it?"

"Yes, but…"

"Listen Daisy," Sarah interrupted. "Stop worrying. You can go to school just as you are…"

"No, Mum, I can't. Not like this."

"Will you listen to me? I know I should have told you before but last week I went to see Mr Horsfall…"

"You went to see Donkeydrop?"

"Yes. Please let me finish. I explained to him that you were having gender identity problems and he suggested that it would probably be best if, in the future, you attended school as a girl…"

"He *suggested* that?"

"Yes. So we agreed that you should take a day off school on Monday. He will make an announcement at assembly in the morning about your change of gender and then you can return to school on Tuesday, but in girls' uniform."

Dan shook his head. "I can't believe this." He could feel his anger rising. "How could you do this without telling me?" he hissed. "I'm not ready. I need more time…"

He was interrupted by the ping of the salon door opening. He turned towards the door and to his horror saw a girl in his class step inside. Her name was April, she only lived three or four doors down from Dan's house and they frequently travelled together on the school bus. She looked around the salon, spotted Sarah, smiled and waved. "Hi Mrs Walter," she said. Sarah waved back. April smiled at Dan, too, but showed no sign of recognition.

"How's Dan?" she asked.

Sarah grinned mischievously. "Why don't you ask him yourself?" she said.

The girl looked puzzled. "Where is he?"

"Right here," Sarah replied, putting a hand on Dan's shoulder.

April leaned forward to take a closer look. Dan smiled weakly and did a little embarrassed wave with one hand. "Oh… my… God…" she said. "Is that you, Dan?"

Dan nodded. The girl covered her mouth with her hand to hide her shock. "Oh my God," she gushed, "you look awesome, totally awesome. I love your hair…" Her voice tailed off; she had no idea what else to say.

Sarah rescued her. "I should explain. Dan's come in for a make-over because from now on he is going to start living as a girl and from Tuesday next he'll be attending school as a girl. That's right, isn't it, Dan?"

Dan shot his mother a poisonous look and nodded. There was no way he could get out of his mother's plans now.

"By the way," Sarah continued, "his girl's name is Daisy."

"That… is… so… cool," April said. Turning to Dan she said "I've come in to have my hair done and I'm going to ask to have it styled just like yours. It looks fab on you."

"Thank you," Dan, still horribly embarrassed, muttered.

"I'd better get on," April said. "Nice to see you Mrs Walter, and you, too, er, Daisy."

"You too," Sarah said. "Ask if Alison is free to do your hair. She did Daisy's."

"I will. Thank you."

April turned her attention back to the receptionist and Sarah whispered to her son "You do realise, don't you, that when she came into the salon she looked straight at you and had no idea who you were? That's why you're perfectly safe going out and about the way you are. I've got an idea. Why don't we go out and grab some lunch, then hit the shops? I'd like to buy you a new dress for the family visit tomorrow. How does that sound?"

Dan, who felt he had completely lost control of his own life, shrugged.

CHAPTER 10

Toby was home by the time Dan and his mother got back from the shops, laden with packages. He took one look at his brother and muttered "Bloody hell. What have they done to your hair? You look like a girl."

Dan, who had been greatly buoyed up during his shopping trip by the admiring glances he had received from almost every boy he passed, snapped "Is that supposed to be a compliment?"

"No."

Dan was determined to needle his brother. "I've got a new dress to wear tomorrow, do you want to see it?"

"No."

"I thought you might be interested."

"Don't be bloody silly," Toby sneered. "Why would I be interested in your stupid dresses? I'm not a pansy, like you."

Sarah intervened. "Stop bickering, you two. Why can't you try and get on, for a change?"

"Why should I try and get on with a brother who looks like my sister?" Toby whined.

"Well you're just going to have to get used to it," Sarah said. "Daisy will be going to school as a girl from next week."

Toby was shocked. "You're not serious?"

Sarah nodded.

"What's Dad going to say when he finds out?"

Sarah stood directly in front of her younger son so she could look him in the face. "Listen to me carefully, Toby. First of all, it's nothing to do with your father. Secondly, he'll only find out when I decide the time is right to tell him. You are not to say anything to him about what is happening here, do you understand?"

Toby lost it. "You keep asking me if I understand," he shouted, "when I don't understand anything! I don't understand why my brother is wearing a skirt and I don't understand why you want him to…."

"I just want to make it clear to you," Sarah said, interrupting him "that you are to say nothing to your father."

"OK, OK," Toby muttered. "I've got it."

* * * *

Dan had been dreading the visit to his cousins, but the make-over had boosted his confidence enormously. For the first time in his life, he no longer felt like a boy in a dress; he felt like a girl.

When his mother's car drew up outside his Uncle and Aunt's house he guessed that everyone inside would be waiting and watching for their arrival. He was sitting in the front passenger seat next to his mother; Toby was sulking in the back.

He opened the door, swung his legs out together, then stood and pulled down the hem of his skirt. He was wearing a cotton mini dress that his mother had bought for him the day previously, with black tights and ankle boots. Actually, Sarah did not think the dress was very suitable but Dan said he loved it and she did not want to puncture his confidence.

Dan guessed that he was probably being watched from within the house. He casually patted his hair to make sure no strands were awry, adjusted the strap of his shoulder bag, looked up at house and smiled.

As he had anticipated, the whole Evans family had rushed into the front room when someone heard Sarah's car approaching. They stood, initially speechless, staring through the curtained window as Dan emerged from the car.

"Oh my God," someone said. "I don't believe it. That can't be Dan."

"Look at his hair. It's pink and blue."

"He's wearing *tights.*"

"Yeah, but he's got great legs."

"Can anyone see if he's got tits?"

"Nah, flat as a board."

"I can't believe this is happening."

Toby was the last of their visitors to get out of the car.

"Look at Toby, he looks really fed up."

"Well wouldn't you be if your brother suddenly became your sister?"

"Dan's not really his *sister*."

"Well he looks like it."

"Yeah, he certainly looks like a girl, doesn't he?"

When Sarah rang the doorbell, Eve turned to her husband and her sons with one last entreaty. "Please,

please, everyone. Please don't stare at Dan as if he is some kind of freak. You may think he is, but I don't want you to show it. None of us really knows what's going on, but now is the time to be kind and understanding."

In truth, Eve was as astonished as her family by the transformation in her nephew. She thought she probably would not have recognised him if she had passed him in the street. She took a deep breath before she opened the door and said "Hi Sarah, hi Toby, hi Da… well, I guess it's Daisy now isn't it? You look a bit different from when I last saw you. Come on in."

Dan followed his mother and brother into the house - Toby barged in front of him - and they followed Sarah into the sitting room where his uncle and his cousins were waiting. Dan almost laughed when he realised that they seemed more nervous than he was. Charlie broke the ice when he said "I think we're all going to take a little time to get used to this."

"Yeah," Dan said, "me too." And everyone laughed. It was not very long before both families reverted to their normal familiarity, cracking jokes and teasing each other. The boys did their best not to ogle Dan - although it was hard - and while he was aware that he was the target of endless sidelong glances, it did not really bother him. When someone suggested going into the garden to kick a ball about he declined. "I've recently discovered," he said, "that football is not that easy in a tight skirt."

In the garden Toby resolutely refused to answer any questions about his brother and or how he felt about what was happening. "It's nothing to do with me," was all he kept saying. He laughed and shrugged his shoulders when one cousin asked him where Dan hid his dick. "I kept looking at his crotch when he wasn't looking and honestly there's not even a hint of a bulge, even in that skirt. It's got to go somewhere. Where does it go?"

After the boys had gone, Sarah and her sister disappeared in to the kitchen, leaving Dan alone with his uncle. "I hope you don't mind, but I think I'm going to have to call you Dan for a bit," he said, "until I get used to this new situation." Dan laughed and said that was fine. "I'd love you tell me what is going on," his uncle continued, "if you feel you can."

Dan had always liked his Uncle Charlie and was relieved to be able to talk someone other than his mother and brother. He told him the whole story, every detail, from starting to wear his dead sister's clothes to having a make-over the previous day in his mother's beauty salon and how his mother had arranged for him to go back to school as a girl in a couple of days. Charlie listened intently, only occasionally interrupting with a question. When Dan had finished, Charlie took his hand and looked at him intently. "You obviously make a very pretty girl," he said, "there's no denying that. But there's just one thing I want to be reassured about and it's this. Are you sure you know what you are doing?"

The question completely threw Dan. As he floundered in his mind for an answer he began to realise that no, he had no idea what he was doing or how things would end up. To his uncle's concern, he suddenly started to cry, big mascara-laden tears rolling down his cheeks. Charlie was mortified. "I'm so sorry," he said. "I really didn't mean to upset you. Forget it."

"It's not you, Uncle," Dan said. "I'm a bit of an emotional mess at the moment. I'm sorry." He reached into his bag for a tissue and carefully wiped his eyes to avoid further smearing his eye make up. Charlie was amazed how every gesture, every movement he made, was that of a girl.

Meanwhile in the kitchen Eve was still voicing her misgivings. "OK, he looks like a girl and acts like a girl, but he's not a girl, is he? It seems to me that by encouraging him the way you have been doing you are storing up trouble for the future."

Sarah tried to keep her temper. She did not want to fall out with her sister, in her sister's house, when everyone else was being so nice about Daisy. She was amazed that the boys had been so polite and had not made crude jokes or asked crude questions. They had treated him like a girl and she was grateful for that. "Look Eve," she said, "Dan is in charge of his own future. If, when he gets to be 18, he decides to have sexual reassignment surgery, that's up to him. If he decides just to be a cross dresser, that's also up to him. And if he decides he wants to go back to being a man, that's also up to him. I'm not going to pressure him any which way."

Eve privately thought her sister was being ingenuous. She was certain that Dan would not be dressing as a girl were it not for the encouragement of his mother, but she kept her counsel.

Later that night, when her sister and nephews had gone and the boys had all disappeared to their rooms, they settled down with a drink - chilled Chardonnay for Eve, Scotch for Charlie - to discuss Sarah's visit. It had been a surreal experience for both of them to find their nephew transformed into a thoroughly convincing - and pretty - girl. Charlie remained convinced that it was something to do with Sarah's grief over the death of Alice and both were very concerned that Dan's father knew nothing about what was going on. They were aware that Sarah's relationship with her ex-husband was toxic and she had made it clear that she did not want him to know what was going on. "When the time it's right I'll tell him," she had said, "but not before." She did not give them a clue as to when the time would be right.

After a long and agonising discussion they could not agree about what to do. Charlie was all for alerting his former brother-in-law. "I never really liked him much," he confessed, "but he is Dan's father and as such has certain rights, despite what Sarah thinks. How can we justify staying silent when his oldest son is being turned into a girl?"

Before he went to bed, Charlie sat at the desk in his study and tapped out a draft message to Tristram:

Hi Tris,

I hope you are prospering in NYC. I thought long and hard - and discussed it at length with Eve - about whether I should send you this e-mail. In the end, I decided it was my duty to make contact with you, as Dan's father.

We think you should know that Dan, with the worrying encouragement of his mother, is now dressing as a girl and living 24/7 as a girl and will apparently start school later this week as a girl. We saw him for the first time in his new gender today, when he came for tea with his mother and Toby. We knew in advance it was going to happen and Eve had pleaded with the boys not to make a fuss and not to embarrass Dan.

None of us knew quite what to expect and none of us anticipated what transpired - that Dan seemed perfectly confident dressed as a girl and was not only entirely convincing but actually very pretty. (He had apparently had his hair styled in Sarah's salon the previous day!) I was able to have a long chat with him while the boys were in the garden and Eve and Sarah were in the kitchen. Apparently it all started when he began cross-dressing in Alice's clothes while no one was in the house. When he was discovered by his mother returning home unexpectedly, she decided to buy him female clothes of his own - an entire wardrobe in fact - and allow him to continue cross-dressing at home. Since then she has done everything in her power to facilitate Dan's transition. My belief is that she is doing this in part to assuage her grief at Alice's untimely death and in part to resurrect Alice - or an Alice figure - in her life. I should emphasise this is only my belief, but it does seem to make sense of her attitude and her enthusiasm to persuade Dan to swap his gender. Frankly, I do not believe Dan would be living as a girl today if it were not for his mother.

It may be, of course, that you are not bothered by all the above, but I think at least you have the right to know about it.

Best wishes.

Charlie."

Charlie showed it to his wife, who pleaded with him not to send it. "I can't betray my sister," she said. "She will never forgive me."

Later, Charlie would bitterly regret listening to her.

* * * * *

Sarah was delighted with the way the visit to her sister's had gone and was proud of her eldest son. She had imagined he would be crippled by embarrassment wearing a dress in the presence of his cousins and was amazed how cool he was. It was as if he had set out to charm everyone and show them that he could not only pass as a girl but was *comfortable* as a girl. By the time they came to leave everyone seemed to have forgotten he was a boy and the cousins lined up to give him a chaste kiss on the cheek as they said goodbye. Even her sister, who made no secret of her private disapproval of what was happening, had to admit that Dan was a very convincing girl. All in all, Sarah had achieved everything she had set out to achieve: her immediate and closest family were now prepared to accept that Dan was going to become Daisy.

The next big step was getting him ready for school. She was planning to take the day off on Monday to take him out and buy his new uniform. She was also hoping she could one day persuade him to ditch all his boys' clothes and perhaps take them to a charity shop. It would be a deeply symbolic gesture if she could get him to agree, but it would be dependant, she thought, on his mood when he woke on Monday morning.

Somewhat to her surprise - she thought he would be getting anxious about school - Dan was remarkably cheerful when he showed up at the breakfast table in a short pleated skirt on Monday morning. In truth, he was still perked up by the events of the day before. He had been dreading, truly dreading, visiting his cousins in a dress, but in the end he had actually *enjoyed* it. He discovered, with a shiver of pleasure, the power that a pretty girl could exert over pubescent boys. He liked the way they kept looking at him - slyly, obviously hoping he would not notice, but he did - with a mixture of awe, wonder and intrigue. He had imagined that they would giggle at his appearance and crack silly jokes, but they did not. He liked the way they looked at his legs when his skirt rode up a little. He liked the way he could flutter his eyelash extensions. He liked being able to toss his hair. He liked the way they began competing for his attention. It was amazing to him that after such a short time, because of the way he looked, they were already treating him like a girl, even though they all knew he was a boy. He still got a bit of a shock every time he looked at himself in the mirror, but it was a nice shock.

He had forgiven his mother for bulldozing him into the visit and for rushing off to talk to Donkeydrop before he was ready. After all, as she kept saying, if he was going to live as a girl he might as well get on with it. What was the point of waiting?

As he was helping his mother clear away the breakfast dishes (Toby had already left for school) she broached the subject of abandoning his boys' clothes and to her delight he instantly agreed that it was a good idea, although he said he did not think any charity shop would be interested. In truth, his former wardrobe only comprised his boys' school uniform, a few pairs of scruffy jeans and a variety of over-worn T-shirts and sweat shirts. They decided to dump the whole lot in a recycling bin on their way to the shops.

Sarah had a complete list of everything he would need - pleated tartan skirts, white blouses, V-neck jumpers, black tights, a bolero jacket and sensible shoes (maximum 2-inch heel). Discreet make-up was allowed (no nail varnish) but no body piercing, except for ear lobes. It was all available in a dusty shop in one of the back streets of Brighton, where an elderly lady made it clear she did not need to be told what it was they wanted once she had taken Dan's waist measurement and shuffled back and forth pulling packages from drawers and piling them onto the counter.

"Just moved into the area have you?" she asked.

"No," Sarah replied, puzzled by the question.

"Oh, changed schools then?"

Suddenly the penny dropped. "Er, yes that's right," she said, nudging Dan, who was starting to giggle.

Later, when they were having lunch at Terre a Terre, Sarah's favourite vegetarian restaurant, she told him she was tempted to tell the old girl the truth ("No, actually this is my son, but he's going back to school as a girl") to see how she would react. Dan laughed and said he was glad she managed to resist the temptation. At that moment his telephone buzzed. He rummaged around in his handbag, desperately trying to find it (he was still having difficulty with handbags) and when he had fished it out he saw it was his friend April calling.

"Daisy, you'll never guess what's happened," she said excitedly when he connected the call, "Donkeydrop's made me one of your mentors! Me and Muriel Gove (another girl with whom Dan was friendly). We're to stick by your side for your first month here as a girl and we're to report directly to Donkeydrop if anyone gives you any trouble. Isn't that great?"

Without giving him a chance to answer, she rushed on "The whole school was, like, blown away, when Donkeydrop made the announcement at the Assembly that a pupil would be switching from the trouser uniform to the skirt uniform. At first he did not say who it was, but everyone knew it was you. Is it OK if I drop by your place on the way home and I'll tell you everything? I've gotta go because I'm late for PE. 'Bye Daisy." Before he was able to reply she had gone. "April's been made one of my mentors," he explained to his mother. "Is it OK if she comes by after school?" Of course, Sarah said.

At home Dan modelled his new uniform at the request of his mother. He changed in his bedroom and when he came downstairs he looked so much like Alice - who had exactly the same uniform - that she started to weep. She did not want to, she just couldn't stop herself. Dan, alarmed, said "What's the matter Mum? Is something wrong" Sarah hastily wiped away her tears and said "No, nothing, nothing at all. I'm just being silly. You look adorable." She took a deep breath and forced a smile. "Just one thing,. I think you'll find your skirt is longer than the other girls. You should probably roll it up at the waistband like everyone does."

He was still in his uniform when April banged on the door. She did not appear to notice and the two of them disappeared into Dan's bedroom for an hour. Sarah did not intervene; she was just so happy - and amazed - that Dan seemed to be taking everything in his stride.

While they were still upstairs Toby arrived home in a foul mood. "Everyone knows now!" he shouted at his mother.

"Knows what, dear?" Sarah asked, pretending innocence.

"YOU KNOW! That *thing,* who is supposed to be my brother, is going back to school tomorrow as my *sister*. Donkeydrop announced it at assembly. I don't know how you can do this to me. I don't want anything to do with any of this, I've never wanted anything to do with this. I don't want a brother who pretends to be a girl. I'm not going to go on the bus with him, I'm not going to talk to him…"

"JUST SHUT UP TOBY!" His mother had to shout to interrupt him. "When will you understand that this is not about you? Why can't you try to understand what is going on here. Daisy needs…"

"DAISY! DAISY! I'm fucking sick of hearing about Daisy. I don't know any fucking Daisy. I hate you and I hate him or her or whatever the fuck he/she is. All I know is that you are destroying our family."

Toby picked up his backpack and stormed out, slamming the door behind him.

Sarah sighed. Well, she said to herself, I always knew it would be difficult.

CHAPTER 11

It was on Tuesday morning, as Dan was slowly getting ready for school, that his nerves kicked in. He had showered, done his make-up (discreetly) and brushed his hair. He could feel his heart thumping as he sat on the bed in his knickers and picked up a pair of tights and pulled them on. At his mother's suggestion he was wearing a white cotton training bra (his nipples had been sore lately and she said a training bra would help, which it did). He buttoned up his blouse, then stepped into his skirt and zipped it up. He stood in front of the mirror as he rolled up the waistband, wondering how far he could go.

At that moment he was suddenly overwhelmed with self-doubt. What was he doing? How could he possibly go back as a girl to the school he had been attending for several years as a boy? He'd be singled out as a freak. Everyone would stare at him and point and jeer. He felt all the colour drain from his face. and his knees went weak. He sat back down on his bed. He couldn't go through with it. He was mad to attempt it, to even think about it. He wished he hadn't agreed to dump all his boys' clothes. If he had his old school uniform he could go back to being boy. But of course he couldn't. How could he be a boy with his pink and blue hair and his fringe and his threaded eyebrows and his lustrous eyelashes? And anyway Donkeydrop had told everyone he would be wearing the "skirt uniform". He was trapped.

    He heard the front door bell ring and knew it would be April, coming to collect him. He was shivering and felt sick. Very slowly he pulled himself to his feet and made his way downstairs, feeling as if he was going to the scaffold. His mother had already let April in. She smiled up at him. "You OK?" she asked chirpily. "Nervous?"

Dan nodded. "You bet. I think I'm going to be sick."

"Nah, you'll be fine."

Dan's mother appeared from the kitchen, smiled broadly and gave Dan a hug. "My pretty schoolgirl," she said. "Are you sure you don't want me to drive you both to school?" She had made the offer the previous evening, but both Dan and April thought it would be better if they took the school bus, as usual. Dan was not at all sure now that it was a good idea, but April interceded.

"Thanks Mrs Walter. We'll be fine. We should get going, Daisy."

Dan nodded, reluctantly picked up his backpack and turned to kiss his mother goodbye. "Good luck, sweetheart," she whispered in his ear. "I'll need it," he mumbled gloomily.

Sarah watched them as they set off up the road. No one would ever guess, she thought proudly, that one of those two schoolgirls was not quite what she seemed.

Dan's heart started thumping hard again as they turned the corner and saw a bigger crowd than usual waiting at the bus stop. His step faltered. If he could have run away he would have done so. As they approached he saw all the boys standing in a little group, leering at him and smirking and whispering together. To his surprise, the girls came running up to him, apparently excited and delighted that he had chosen to join their number. They peppered him with questions about how long he had been dressing as a girl and why and how and what his Mum thought...

It continued on the bus, where he sat surrounded by girls. It was the same when they arrived at school - all the boys ignored him and all the girls wanted to talk to him. He only extricated himself when someone told him he had to report to Donkeydrop before he started lessons.

He had to wait 15 minutes outside the headmaster's study, enduring the unwelcome attention of the school secretary, an ugly spinster who covertly gawked at him while pretending to be working at her computer.

When he was finally ushered into the head's study, Donkeydrop looked him up and down with evident curiosity. Dan was obliged to stand meekly in front of his desk as the headmaster launched into a long speech about how proud he was that Downs Comprehensive had led the way introducing gender choice regarding trouser uniforms and skirt uniforms, but that the policy was a privilege not a right and could be withdrawn at any time, if it caused too much disruption to the smooth running of the school. Dan would obviously take some time to settle in while wearing the girls' uniform; he was to immediately report any attempts to bully, humiliate or harass him in any way and the perpetrators would be severely punished. Finally, he would be excused from all sporting activities for the time being and was to use the staff facilities until such point that the school had entirely gender-free toilet facilities.

Donkeydrop looked him up and down once again. "Well you certainly look like a girl," he said, "so that will help a lot. Run along now and catch up with your first class."

"Thank you sir," Dan said. He turned and walked out through the outer office; the unsmiling secretary sniffed her obvious disapproval as he passed her desk. He hurried along the corridors to his classroom, where one of his favourite teachers, Miss Ransom, was taking history. When he knocked on the door and walked in, there was an immediate commotion, a burst of giggles and mumbling which Miss Ransom silenced immediately by banging on her desk. "Good morning, Daisy," she said, entirely unperturbed, as if boys often walked in dressed as girls. "Please take a seat." April had reserved a place for him at the desk next to hers and Dan gratefully slid into the seat, instinctively brushing his skirt under his bottom as he did so.

"Well, you've all had a good look now." Miss Ransom said, addressing the class. "You obviously all know who she was, but that is in the past. Daisy is now a girl…"

"Some girl!" someone called out, causing a ripple of sniggers.

Miss Ransom sighed. "I'll let that pass, just this once. Any more sarcastic remarks like that will result in the person involved being sent to the Head. Is that clear?" There was a mumble of assent. "Good. Now let's get back to work."

By lunchtime the worst was over. Dan became used to boys muttering "freak" as he passed them in the corridors, but it did not greatly bother him and most of the girls were wonderfully supportive. April and his other mentor, Muriel Gove, stuck closely by his side and during the lunch break they sat together, ignoring the boys cracking crude jokes at the next table.

Nevertheless, Dan was mightily relieved when the bell signalled the end of the school day.

* * * * *

Three weeks after Dan had started school as a girl, Sarah received the first of several visits from the Social Services. She answered a hesitant knock on her front door to find two mousey women with photo IDs on lanyards round their necks on her doorstep. They flashed their IDs and introduced themselves as child protection officers carrying out a Section 47 Enquiry.

"What's that when it's at home?" Sarah asked flippantly.

"If there are concerns about the safety or welfare of a child," one of the women intoned, as if reading from a script, "we carry out what is called a Section 47 Enquiry to ensure the needs of the child are being met."

"And why would you possibly think the needs of my children are *not* being met?" Sarah asked, her voice heavy with sarcasm.

"Mrs Walter, I think it might be better if we discussed this inside, don't you?"

Sarah opened the door wider and with exaggerated courtesy ushered the women into the hall. Then she shut the door, leaned against it and surveyed her visitors. She decided that somehow or the other Tristram had discovered what was going on and was causing trouble. "It's my former husband, isn't it?" she snapped. "He's reported me, hasn't he? That's why you're here."

"I'm sure you know we are not at liberty to discuss that."

"No, of course you are not," Sarah snorted angrily. "But I'm at liberty to tell you that the bastard to whom I was once unfortunately married and who is the father of my children is a homophobic, chauvinistic, misogynistic bigot without an ounce of decency in his…"

The speaking woman interrupted her. "Mrs Walter, is there somewhere we can sit and talk?"

Sarah led them into the kitchen and pointed to the chairs at the kitchen table. Both of them sat down, took files and notebooks out of their briefcases and set them on the table. Sarah did not offer them coffee or water; she wanted them out of the house as soon as possible. It soon became clear, as she suspected, that the focus of their attention was Dan; they did not seem the least bit interested in Toby.

Only one of the women seemed to have a tongue. "It is our understanding that your older son, Dan, is currently living as a woman. Is that correct?"

Sarah laughed. "Not a woman, exactly. A girl, yes."

"Is that his choice?"

"Of course it's his bloody choice!" Sarah exploded. "What a bloody ridiculous question! You can't make a 16-year-old boy dress as a girl unless he wants to."

The woman ignored her rudeness. "And how did this come about?"

Sarah sighed and launched into a description of how Dan had started cross-dressing in secret and how it had all developed to the point where he was now living as a girl and even attending school as a girl. Both women took detailed notes as she was speaking. When she had finished, the woman who had done all the speaking nodded to her colleague, as if to say "Take over."

"Mrs Walter," the second woman said. "Dan started cross-dressing in his dead sister's clothes. Is that correct?"

"Yes."

"Can I ask you why you kept her clothes for so long after her unfortunate accident?"

Sarah could feel her temperature rising. "No you can't. It's nothing to do with you."

"I see. Do you think, by dressing in his sister's clothes, Dan was trying in some subconscious way to bring her back, or at least bring the memory of her back?"

"No, I don't."

"What about you, Mrs Walter?"

"What about me?"

"Does Dan, or Daisy as he now is, help you recover from the grief of your lost child."

Sarah knew it would be unwise to lose her temper in front of these two women, but she was finding it increasingly hard. "Have you ever lost a child?" she demanded.

"I don't have any children."

"Well let me tell you this. You can never, ever, recover from the grief. It stays with you every second, and every minute, of every hour, every day. Having Dan living as Daisy does nothing, *nothing*, to help. No matter what psycho-babble shit my husband has fed you, that's the truth."

This outburst seemed to satisfy them for the moment, because they then asked, to Sarah's surprise, if they could see Dan's bedroom. She shrugged. "If you want." She led them upstairs, opened Dan's door and nodded for them to enter. She could see their eyebrows shooting up as they looked around. It was indisputably a girls' room: the boy band posters on the wall, a nightdress draped across the bed; underwear and a pair of tights left on the carpet, the make-up scattered over the top of the dressing table, a hair drier still plugged in. The wardrobe doors were open, revealing dresses and skirts jammed on a rack and a jumbled pile of shoes at the bottom.

"Does he not have any boys' clothes?"

"No," Sarah replied, "Daisy wanted to throw them all out as soon as she had transitioned full time."

"That was his decision?"

Sarah was irritated by the way they kept using male pronouns. "*Hers*. Yes."

She was taken aback by their next question. "Can we see Alice's room now?"

"Why?"

One of them mumbled something about the "family dynamic", but Sarah wasn't buying it. She shook her head and said she did not want anyone rooting around among Alice's things and anyway she had to get back to work, so if they were finished… They said they would need to return to interview Dan and Toby out of school time and Sarah said fine why did they not ring her to make an appointment and hustled them out through the front door.

As she closed it behind them she breathed a sigh of relief. She would never, never forgive her former husband for her putting her through this. How had he found out? No one at the school would know how to contact him; it could only have been her sister or her brother-in-law or, unlikely, one of their kids. She picked up her mobile and punched her sister's number. She picked up immediately.

"Eve, I've just had the Social Services round," Sarah said. "I think Tristram must have found out about Daisy and reported me. You didn't tell him, did you?"

"Of course not," Eve replied. "You asked us not to."

"What about Charlie?"

"No. He does think Tristram has the right to know but I pleaded with him to keep your confidence and I'm sure he would not betray you."

What Eve did not tell her sister was that it was Charlie who had contacted the Social Services. "If we are not going to tell Tristram," he had said, "someone needs to keep a check on what Sarah is doing to prevent her screwing up Dan's life completely."

Eve, very reluctantly, had agreed.

* * * * *

Dan was alarmed when, that evening, Sarah told him the Social Services were taking an interest in the family and that he would have to be interviewed. "What do they want?" he demanded. "What's wrong? Why do I have to talk to them?

Sarah had thought long and hard about how much to tell him and how to reassure him. She told him not to worry, it was just that the Social Services had got the ridiculous idea that he was being forced to dress as a girl against his wishes and that she was somehow involved.

"But why would they think that?" Dan persisted.

Sarah shook her head. "I honestly don't know. Probably just some busy body trying to interfere in our lives."

They sat in silence for a moment, then Dan said, as if he was reading his mother's mind, "Do you think it is something to do with Dad? Do you think he has found out?"

Since talking to her sister Sarah had come to believe that it could not be her former husband who had reported her to the Social Services. If he had somehow found out about Daisy he would have been on the telephone immediately, shouting and swearing at her and demanding an explanation. It was not his style to sneak behind her back or miss an opportunity to criticise her and tell her she was a "fucking useless human being" and "a hopeless mother". Discovering that she was encouraging Dan to dress as a girl would be a perfect opportunity for him to try and prove she was unstable and seek custody of the children, a threat he was always holding over her.

"No," she said, "I am pretty sure your father knows nothing. Look, sweetie, don't keep worrying about it. All you have to do is let them know that you are dressing the way you are because you want to and not because I am making you." Sarah managed an ironic laugh too emphasise how ridiculous such a notion was.

But Dan did keep worrying about it. He had heard any number of scare stories about the heavy-handed tactics of the Social Services, of children being taken into care into unnecessarily. On the night before the "terrible twins" - as Sarah had taken to calling them - were due to turn up at his house to interview him he had tearfully asked his mother if he was going to be taken away. "No," she replied forcefully. "No one is going to take you away. You have done nothing wrong and neither have I. Stop fretting. You'll be fine."

And he was. Sarah had insisted on being present during the interview and she could see the astonishment on their faces when Dan entered the room. He had changed out of his school uniform into a pretty pink cotton mini dress which suited him wonderfully well. He had put his hair in plaits, which made him look younger than he was, and his make-up was perfect, but discreet. He looked, Sarah thought, utterly gorgeous; a girl through and through. As he sat down, brushing his skirt under his bottom, his knees pressed together, she caught the way the "terrible twins" exchanged glances as if to say *"This is a boy?"*

It was obvious Dan was nervous and he answered their questions as briefly as he could, sometimes in monosyllables. He only became flustered when they started asking him about the extent to which his cross-dressing had been influenced by his mother. First he prevaricated. "I'm not sure what you mean."

"Did she encourage you to wear girls' clothes?"

"Not really."

"Didn't she buy you your first wardrobe?"

"Yes."

"Well wasn't that encouragement?"

"Not really."

"OK. Let's call it helping. Why do you think she helped you?"

"She's always helped me…"

The questioning went on for another hour, with Dan stubbornly refusing to accept that his mother had anything to do with his choice of gender. Sarah did not intervene. She could see he was doing well and she could see that his interlocutors were not making any headway. Only at the very end did she hold her breath when one of the "terrible twins" asked, very quietly, about his dead sister.

"Daisy, has it ever occurred to you that your mother might be encouraging you to dress like a girl to replace the daughter she lost, your sister Alice?"

Dan did not speak for what seemed an age. For most of the interview he had refused to look at his questioners, but he lifted his eyes to stare directly at them and then he said, equally quietly: "No, that has never occurred to me." He paused, then added "Ever."

Sarah wanted to jump up and hug him.

When the "terrible twins" returned to talk to Toby they made the big mistake of telling him that he did not need to answer their questions if he did not want to. "Fine," he said, "then I won't." With that he crossed his arms over his chest and pressed his lips tightly together. He did not even open them to say goodbye. Sarah could not stop herself grinning.

Four weeks later she received a formal letter from Brighton Social Services informing her that the Section 47 Enquiry relating to her son, Daniel James Walter, also known as Daisy Walter, had been closed and that no further action would be taken.

CHAPTER 12

After Dan's debut as Daisy at his Aunt Eve's house, word had quickly spread around the family about what was happening. Reactions varied. Some of Sarah's more elderly relatives made no secret of their shock and horror, disgust even. "How could you possibly allow him to do something so ridiculous? I certainly do not want to see Dan in a dress," one elderly aunt wrote to Sarah. Younger relatives were more tolerant, more intrigued, and took to stopping by at Sarah's house as they "just happened" to be in the area. Sarah knew - and Dan knew - that all they wanted was to take a look at Dan.

Dan, increasingly confident as a girl, tolerated these intrusive family visits with reasonably good grace and enjoyed the many compliments he received, even if some were back-handed. "You could almost be a girl," one cousin told him, unintentionally making Dan laugh.

Sarah thought that Toby had at last become reconciled to Dan being Daisy. For the first month he would not address a word to his brother, not a word, but bit by bit he softened. As Daisy became accepted at school a simply another girl - very few boys bothered to mutter "freak" any more when they passed him in the corridor - so he became accepted by his brother at home. It was not long before Toby began using female pronouns - "she" and "her" when referring to Dan - and Sarah knew the battle had been won when she overheard Toby introducing a new friend to Dan as "my sister Daisy". Later, when Sarah thanked him, he just shrugged his shoulders and mumbled "It's easier."

Three months after he began taking daily "vitamin" pills, Dan noticed he was beginning to grow boobs; not full blown tits, but very definite mounds on his chest, with enlarged nipples. He Googled "boys with breasts" and discovered there was a common condition called *gynecomastia* which caused some teenage boys to grow breasts. He mentioned it to his mother and she, concealing her delight, went out and bought him a selection of the prettiest laciest 32AA bras she could find to replace the training bras he had been wearing since starting school as Daisy.

April, Dan's new best friend and neighbour, was obsessed with finding him a boyfriend. She talked about it constantly during school breaks and when they hung out together at weekends, often with other girls from Downs Comprehensive. Dan kept saying he did not want a boyfriend, but April did not believe him. "'Course you do," she said. "Every girl wants a boyfriend."

"But I'm not every girl, am I?" Dan retorted.

"Good as," April replied with a sly smile.

The truth was that Dan was longing to have a boyfriend, but he had been scarred by the incident with Mark, up on the Downs, when he had narrowly avoided being raped. He remembered, however, how much he had enjoyed walking hand in hand with Mark along the seafront, how much he had enjoyed being kissed, how much he had enjoyed Mark's company before he had turned nasty. Whenever he thought about what had happened he usually blamed himself; he should have told Mark from the outset that he was a boy and then there would not have been any misunderstanding. But if he'd done that, would Mark have wanted to see him? He had no idea, but he thought probably not.

It was at an 18th birthday party - April's older brother - that he met James. He had not wanted to go to the party, but April had insisted and had offered to lend him a dress - a silver lame sheath with bootlace straps - he really liked. They got ready together in April's bedroom - she was completely unbothered by the sight of his genitals, although he did his best to conceal them - and travelled together in a taxi to the party, which was being held in a basement nightclub on the seafront. Both of them were made up to the nines with ultra smokey eyes, wearing very short skirts and very high heels.

When they made an entrance, every eye turned in their direction. April's brother had known Dan before his transition but now always treated him like a girl. "My God you two," he said as he greeted them, "I've never seen you both looking so glamorous. I'm honoured."

"It's not for you, bruv," April said, punching him on the arm. "We're going to a real party later on."

"You wish," he replied.

Despite himself, Dan enjoyed the party. The DJ was great and lots of boys wanted to dance with him, although after about an hour he had to take off his heels - they were killing him. April followed suit and they both continued dancing in their tights, flinging themselves about the dance floor like mad things. One or two boys tried to kiss Dan on the lips, but he moved his head aside to offer them a cheek. April laughed when she saw what he was doing. "Oh my," she said "Miss Modesty. Shall I show you how it's done?"

She grabbed the boy she was dancing with, pulled his head towards her and planted her open mouth on his with the force of a suction pump. He was so surprised that he drew back and they both fell to the floor, giggling hysterically.

Shortly before midnight, when Dan was due to return home, he realised that April was missing. He looked everywhere for her - including the Ladies - and eventually found her outside, at the back of the club, with her skirt round her waist having sex with a boy against a wall. He was so shocked that he rushed back inside, ran through the club and out onto the seafront basement, planning to call a cab to take him home. He fished his phone out of his handbag only to discover it had no charge. He swore under his breath.

It was at that moment that he realised someone, a boy, had followed him out of the club. "Hello," he said, "are you OK?"

Dan grimaced. "Not really. I've got to get home and I've just discovered my phone has run out of juice. Can I borrow yours?"

"I can do better than that. I can take you home. My car's only just round the corner."

Dan was suspicious. "Have you been drinking or taking anything?"

The boy laughed. "No. I'm not that stupid. I never drink or smoke when I'm driving. Promise. My name's James, by the way."

"Daisy."

"OK, Daisy. Would you like a lift, or not?"

Dan nodded gratefully. "Thank you. That would be great. I don't live far away, but too far to walk in these heels." Dan bent a leg at the knee to show his high heels.

James laughed. "Yeah, I can imagine. OK. Let's go."

He held out a hand to Dan to help him up the stairs to street level, then released his hand as they walked side by side in silence a few paces along the seafront to a side road where James used his remote to unlock the doors of a new Cooper Mini. He held open the passenger door for Dan, who was now perfectly accustomed to getting in and out of cars in a tight skirt. He slipped into the seat bottom first, then swung his legs in and pulled down the hem of his dress.

James walked round the car, got in to the driver's seat and said "Where to?"

Dan gave him directions and in ten minutes they were parked outside Dan's house. Dan thanked him and was about to get out when James touched his arm and said "Wait. Can I talk to you for a minute?"

Dan looked at his watch. It was five minutes to twelve. "OK," he said.

James hesitated. "You probably didn't realise it, but I was watching you - you and your friend - at the party. It looked like you were having a great time."

"We were. Why didn't you ask me to dance?"

James laughed. "I'm not much of a dancer and I'm a bit shy."

Dan did not know what to say, so they sat in embarrassed silence for a moment or two, both staring out through the windscreen at the darkened street.

Eventually James spoke. "Daisy, do you think I could see you again?"

Dan could feel himself blushing. He knew he was going to have to tell this nice boy his secret. "James," he said, nervously. "There is something about me that you ought to know."

To his surprise, James smiled and said "I know."

"What do you think you know?" he asked.

"I know you're a boy."

Dan swallowed hard. "How do you know?"

"April's brother told me."

Dan felt a surge of anger. April had sworn her brother to secrecy, but before he could say anything James said "There is also something about me you ought to know."

"What's that?"

"I'm gay."

CHAPTER 13

Over the next few weeks, Dan learned a lot about James Mitchison. They had their first date two days after the party, meeting at the pier and going for a walk along the seafront and a coffee at Lucky Beach cafe. James was a perfect gentleman, very polite and caring, treating Dan, as Daisy, with respect. He was too shy to talk much about himself at the beginning, but seemed fascinated by Dan's story and wanted every detail about how he had transitioned. It took him some time to pluck up the courage to hold Dan's hand and even longer to kiss him.

    Dan told his mother about his new friend, that he was gay and knew about Dan and so there would be no nasty surprises. Sarah seemed happy about the relationship and insisted on meeting James the first time he came to collect Dan at the house. She professed herself to be charmed. "What a nice boy," she said to Dan later, "and he's obviously very keen on you." Dan, as always, blushed deeply.

Bit by bit, Dan learned about James' troubles. His family was very well off - his father, Gary, was a builder and property developer who had made a lot of money. James was an only child and was frequently lonely. The family lived in a large house with a swimming pool overlooking the sea in Rottingdean, outside Brighton. His mother, Gloria, was a glamorous former model his father proudly described as his "trophy wife." James was at a loss to understand how she could ever have married him.

When James came out to his mother she was kind and sympathetic but she warned him that his father must never know. "Never, never! Do you understand?" she had said. James understood only too well. Gary Mitchison was a bigot, a racist and a virulent homophobe.

He would stand at the bar at his golf club railing against "poofs" and "dykes". "So-called" same sex marriages, he declared frequently, were unnatural and against God's law, although he had not seen the inside of a church since he married Gloria. He often voiced his gratitude to his friends at the golf club that his son was as "straight as a dye" and confessed he did not know what he would do if he turned out to be a "queer".

So it was that at home James had to live a lie, laugh at his father's tasteless jokes about "shirt-lifters" and "bum bandits" and pretend , as his father asserted to his friends, that he was a "chip off the old block". His father was always nagging him to find a girl friend, to which James would always reply, untruthfully, that he had a lot of a girl friends. "OK, but how many are you fucking?" his father inquired. "You're missing the best shagging days of your life. When I was your age I had lost count of how many shags I had had. Sometimes it was two or three a night…"

James was obliged to sit and listen while his father described, in graphic, lascivious detail, his sexual adventures as a young stud. "Sometimes I think I am going to be physically sick," he confessed to Dan, when they were sitting side by side, holding hands, on a bench on the seafront. "Why does he think I would be interested? It's disgusting."

The arrival of "Daisy" into James' life meant at last that he could tell his father he had a "girl friend" he was dating regularly.   "What's she look like?" he demanded. "Is she a looker?"

"Definitely," James replied.

"You fucking her?"

"Dad!"

James' mother raised an eyebrow when she heard about "Daisy" and she wondered what was coming when, while his father was out of the house, he said there was something he had to tell her. She assumed that her son had acquired a girl friend for no other reason than to please his father and she speculated how long it would be before the girl found out that her new boy friend was gay.

"Mum, about Daisy," he began. "I'm not quite sure how to tell you this, but she is not quite what she seems…"

Gloria was intrigued. "In what way?"

"Well… well… well…" James could not find the words.

"Come on darling," his mother prompted, "out with it."

James took a deep breath and blurted out "Daisy's a boy!"

Gloria was stunned into silence while she digested this information. "Does she look like a boy?" she asked after a moment.

James laughed. "No, no, no, not at all. You would never guess, ever, that she was a boy. She looks, and acts, exactly like a girl. I mean, she lives, full time as a girl, goes to school as a girl. She *is* a girl, except she's not, if you see what I mean."

"Well, not really…." she paused, then inquired "Is this a serious relationship?"

James thought about his mother's question then said "I'm not sure, but I think it might be. We've only been going out together a little while, but we get on really, really well and I like her very, very much."

"Have you, er, been intimate?"

"Mum! You're as bad as Dad!"

"Well, have you?"

James looked embarrassed. "Well, not really. I mean we sort of fondle each other when we can, when no one's looking…"

"OK, OK, I don't need to know the details. Firstly, I don't have to tell you that your father must never, ever, find out about this Daisy's true identity. I don't know what he would do if he did, but it would not surprise me if he disowned you and threw you out of the house. Secondly, I want to meet Daisy and make sure for myself that, as you say, she can pass as a girl. If there is anything about her, anything, that might indicate that she is not what she seems than you can never bring her home. You understand that, don't you…"

Later that night, Gloria Mitchison sat at her dressing table taking off her make-up in front of the mirror - she and her husband had had separate bedrooms for years - and worrying about her son's latest bombshell. She found it hard to believe that a 16-year-old boy could pass scrutiny as a girl. It was hard enough for James to hide his sexuality from his father, but she brooded that this relationship, if it truly was a relationship, would only increase the risks of exposure.

    She sighed. Her son was the only light in her life. If she had ever loved her husband - and frankly she doubted she ever had - she no longer loved him now and had not done so for years. When had they last had sex? She could not remember.

She knew he had a mistress somewhere and she did not give a damn. He could have ten mistresses for all she cared. How much she hated him. She would have left him years ago - soon after James was born in fact - except for the certain knowledge that he would do everything in his power to leave her penniless. All she cared about was James' happiness and as far as she was concerned she was the sole guardian of that. In some ways she was glad he was gay because that meant he was nothing like his brute of a father, but the fear that he would be exposed was always with her.

And now he had found himself a "girlfriend" who was a boy. She sighed again. She doubted if she would get much sleep that night.

* * * * *

Dan was not at all happy when James announced that his mother wanted to meet him. "Why?" he asked immediately.

"Well, I've told her about you and she is obviously intrigued and would like to meet you."

"What do you mean intrigued?"

"Well, I told her the truth."

Dan frowned. "I wish you hadn't done that."

"Daisy, my Mum knows I'm gay. She knows there is zero chance of me having a serious girl friend."

"What about your Dad? What if he finds out?"

"He won't. He'll never know…"

Dan eventually, and reluctantly, agreed to meet James' mother, so long as James was with him. On the morning they were due to meet, Dan dressed with special care; he wanted to make a good impression. He tried on several outfits before he plumped for a denim mini skirt with buttons down the front, a blue and white striped top, black tights and Doc Martens - his default footwear if he was not wearing heels. His mother had bought him several light summer tops, but the outline of his bra was visible with some of them and he did not like that, even though he now had something - well, a little something - to put in a bra.

He was unable to resist putting on too much eye make-up - these days he never left the house without mascara and he'd been reprimanded three times at school for wearing too much. He thought he looked seriously weird without mascara when he looked at himself in the mirror. He pinned his hair up into a loose bun on the top of his head, painted his lips with bright red lipstick and was ready. Any minute now, James would ring the front door bell.

They had arranged to meet at 11 o'clock at the Trading Post, a cafe in the centre of town. Gloria deliberately arrived early and secured a table by the window so that she could see them approach. For some reason, although she was not sure why, she wanted to catch a glimpse of Daisy before she had to meet her. She was surprised to find she was nervous. Suppose it was quite obvious that Daisy was a cross-dressing boy. What was she supposed to do then?

She sat sipping her cortado, anxiously watching the street in both directions. She gasped when, after a few minutes, James appeared around a corner at the end of the street hand in hand with a pretty blonde girl. My God, she thought, that had to be Daisy! How could she possibly be a boy? A wave of relief swept over her that she really did look like a girl.

James held the door open for Dan and Gloria waved at them. Smiling broadly and followed by Dan he walked across to his mother's table and bent over to kiss her cheek. "Mum," he said, pulling Dan forward by the hand, "this is Daisy."

Gloria smiled and put out her hand and Dan shook it. "Nice to meet you Mrs Mitchison," he said politely.

"Gloria, please," she replied. "Sit down my dear. James will get the coffees, won't you darling? I'll have another cortado."

Daisy sat down at the table and James strolled across to join the queue at the counter. Gloria smiled again, unsure how to start a conversation. It was still almost impossible for her to believe that this young person - she was even prettier close up - could possibly be a boy.

"You're very pretty," she said at last. Christ, she thought, she's even prettier when she blushes. (Gloria could not bring herself to use male pronouns.)

Gloria, hesitated, then reached forward and touched Dan's hand. "I've got to ask you this, even though it may seem terribly intrusive and rude. Are you really a boy?"

Dan caught his breath, then nodded.

"Well, no one would ever believe it."

Dan found his voice at last. "I don't know how much James has told you about me…"

"Very little" Gloria interrupted.

"… Well this is what happened." Dan briefly ran through the story of his transition, explaining how his mother had helped him and how he just felt more comfortable as a girl and how everyone, well almost everyone, in the family now accepted him as a girl.

Gloria listened carefully, more and more taken with this strange boy/girl. He was unlike anyone she had ever met and when he had finished talking, she decided to be completely frank. "I don't know how much James has told you about his father…"

"Quite a bit."

"Well you will know then, that it is absolutely essential that he never discovers the truth about you and that he never discovers James is gay. As far as I am concerned, you are a girl and you are James' girl friend. End of. It's obvious you make him happy and that's all I care about…"

At this point James arrived back at their table carrying three coffees. "Everything all right?" he asked anxiously.

CHAPTER 14

Gloria Mitchison was delighted with "Daisy" and thought "she" was the perfect "girlfriend" for her son. A couple of days later she arranged to meet Dan's mother for coffee in town and the two women soon bonded, discussing their respective, equally flawed, husbands and their unusual children . Both agreed that the relationship between Dan and James needed to be encouraged and that it was mutually beneficial to both sides. Gloria suggested that she should bring the children over to her place for lunch next Sunday; it would be a good idea, she said, for her husband to meet Daisy sooner rather than later. Sarah said her younger son would be away playing football, but that she would be happy to come with Daisy. And so it was arranged.

Dan instantly went into panic mode when he heard about the arrangement. "James says his father is a monster," he said to his mother, "if he finds out about me…"

"And how is he going to do that?" his mother demanded. "I'm not going to tell him, Gloria's not going to tell him, you"re not going to tell him and James is certainly not going to tell him. As far as he is concerned you're his son's new girlfriend and that's an end to the matter."

In the privacy of his bedroom later that evening, Dan talked to James for a long time on his phone about how nervous he was about meeting his father. James assured him he had nothing to worry about. "He's so pleased I've got a girl friend at last that he'll be predisposed to like you. And when he sees how pretty you are… all you have to do is flutter your eyelashes and he'll be captivated. He'll probably want to tell you what a success he was with girls when he was a my age, but you'll just have to put up with that and pretend to be interested."

Nevertheless Dan remained nervous and Sarah could sense his tension as they drove out together to the Mitchison house the following Sunday morning, the first real summer day of the year. He was looking, she thought, gorgeous in a red patterned knee-length dress, bare legs (he had had them tanned at the beauty salon the day before) and sneakers. He had his hair pinned up and had even eschewed the heavy eye make-up he normally wore in favour of grey eye shadow and just a touch of mascara.

As they pulled into the drive, she touched his hand and he managed a weak smile. "James will look after you," she said and he nodded uncertainly. They had to wait for a pair of big wooden gates to open electronically and then drove through into a gravel courtyard in front of a huge recently-built house. "Christ" she muttered under her breath, "it's a bloody mansion."

By the time they had got out of the car, Gloria Mitchison and James had emerged from the house to welcome them. "Sarah, Daisy… hello," Gloria said, kissing Sarah on both cheeks and hugging Dan. James went straight to Dan and gave him a discreet kiss on the lips. "You look nice," he said.

Dan, heartened by James' presence, smiled.

"Gary's out the back working the barbecue," Gloria said. "Why don't we go round the side of the house?"

She led the way, talking all the time to Sarah, explaining things about the house. James and Dan followed, hand in hand. "It's going to be fine," James whispered, squeezing Dan's hand. "I hope you are right," he replied.

They turned the corner to find a vast swimming pool with an elaborate gas barbecue set-up at one end and a grossly overweight man, bare-chested, with his stomach drooping over the waistband of Hawaiian shorts, sweating profusely at the grill, flipping burgers.

"Gary," Gloria said, "this is Sarah Walter and her daughter Daisy, James' friend."

Gary put down his barbecue tools. "Welcome," he said, shaking Sarah's outstretched hand. Then he turned to Dan. Looking him up and down with approval he said "Obviously my son's got good taste, just like his father." He threw his head back and roared with laughter.

Dan was not sure what to say, but before he could say anything, James' father had grabbed him in a bear hug which Dan would have thought affectionate were it not for the fact that he could feel the man's erection pressing against his dress. "Mr Mitchison," he gasped, "I can't breathe."

Everyone laughed edgily as Mitchison released him. "It's Gary please," he boomed. "No Mr Mitchisons here. Now what would everyone like to drink?"

Dan slowly began to relax as they all settled in comfortable garden chairs and drinks were served and Gary resumed his station at the smoking barbecue, taking a glass and a bottle of red wine with him. James said little, but kept smiling encouragingly at Dan as their mothers talked.

Gary dominated the conversation at lunch boasting, as James correctly predicted, about the innumerable beautiful women he had dated before he married Gloria and about his success in business and the vast amounts of money he had made. He insisted that Dan sat next to him and insisted that he should have wine with the meal. "You'll have to learn to handle your drink if you want to hang out with this family, won't she James?" James smiled and shrugged.

By the end of the meal - chicken pieces, sausages and sweetcorn, all burned to a crisp on the barbecue followed by strawberries and cream - Dan was feeling distinctly whoozey and was unbothered by Gary's leg pressing against his under the table. He reckoned that James' father had probably drunk at least two bottles of wine and his speech was distinctly slurred as he started telling faintly questionable jokes. Sarah, Dan and James all laughed politely at the punch lines, but Dan noticed that James' mother just stared blankly into space.

Finally it seemed that Gary had run out off jokes because he stood up, somewhat unsteadily, took Dan's hand and said "OK Daisy, you ready for a swim?"

Dan, taken by surprise, shook his head. "I'm sorry, Gary. I don't have a costume."

"Oh we don't bother with costumes," Gary said with a sly look at his wife, who rolled her eyes.

Dan could feel the blood rushing to his head. There was no way he could skinny dip and expose himself to James' father. He opened his mouth to say something when Gary roared with laughter again. "Just kidding" he snorted. "There are plenty of costumes over there" - he pointed to a shepherd's hut on the lawn "and you can change there too."

He paused and gave Dan an appraising look. "Actually, you don't have much on top so you could probably just jump in in your trunks if you wanted to."

Gloria sighed loudly. "Gary please! You're embarrassing her," she said to her husband. "Just stop it." Turning to Dan she said "Daisy, I must apologise for my husband, he has a weird sense of humour."

Gary smirked and spread his arms in an exaggerated gesture of innocence. "I'm not embarrassing you, am I Daisy? Tell me I'm not."

Dan felt himself blushing even more. He smiled and shrugged. In reality he was acutely embarrassed by James' father's remarks, but he did not want to admit it. He was also irritated that the man thought he did "not have much on top" as his breasts had developed rapidly and he had now outgrown the 32AA bras his mother had bought him a few months ago. (He still attributed this to *gynecomastia,* rather than the "vitamin" pills he routinely swallowed every morning at his mother's insistence.)

James spoke up. "If you want to go for a swim, Daisy, I'll go up to my room and change into my shorts, but you don't have to."

Dan thought about it. It was warm and the pool certainly looked very inviting. He tried to calculate the risks. If he could find a bikini with tight pants he could certainly tuck his willy away. His tits wouldn't fill a bikini top but the bra he was wearing would do as a top, worst come to the worst.

He smiled at James. "Yes, let's do it."

"Great," he said. "I'll see you in a few minutes." He ran into the house. Dan got up from the table and walked across to the shepherd's hut, conscious that all three adults were looking at him. He climbed the steps into the hut and shut and locked the door behind him. Inside there were neat piles of swimming costumes and towels stacked on two shelves. He unfastened his dress, slipped his arms out of the sleeves and let it fall to the floor, then took off his sneakers, one by one and stepped out of his knickers. He pulled down several bikinis from the shelf and examined them. Two were too big and too loose, but the third, in black, looked about right - a bottom with imitation bows at each side and top with a halter neck. He stepped into the bottom part, pulled it up to his knees, tucked his willy between his legs and pulled it up fully. Fortunately there was a mirror in the hut and he was able to check how it looked. It was fine and felt completely secure. He reached behind his back to unhook his bra, then tried on the bikini top. The straps were adjustable and he was able to make it fit securely over his little boobs. After one last check in the mirror, he wrapped a towel round himself, unlocked the door and stepped out.

James and his father were already fooling around in the pool, while Sarah and Gloria sat together on adjoining sun loungers, talking and watching what was going on. Sarah was gratified that Dan had emerged with a towel wrapped round his chest, like a girl.

"You know," Gloria said *sotto voce,* "it's very hard to think of Daisy as anything other than a girl."

"That's good," Sarah replied drowsily. She was wondering whether she should drive home when the time came; she had had several glasses of wine.

"You'll have to watch Gary," Gloria continued. 'He's got a penchant for young girls and the fact that she's James' girl friend wouldn't stop him." Sarah, half asleep from the wine, did not react.

Dan had removed his towel and was stepping gingerly into the shallow end of the pool. "Look at her," Gloria said, "she looks fabulous in a bikini."

Sarah had to admit that he did. It was the first time she had seen him in a swimsuit. James had waded across the pool to take his hand and as they got into deeper water he scooped Dan up. Dan put an arm round James' neck and nuzzled into his shoulder. She heard Gary shout "Hey, you two love birds" as he began splashing them with water. With seconds the three of them were engaged in a full-blown water fight, laughing like crazy. Somehow Gary manoeuvred to Dan's side and put an arm, protectively, round his slim waist, while they both focussed on drenching James.

"Look at my oaf of a husband," Gloria whispered. "Any minute now he'll snap her bra strap." To Sarah's surprise, she was right. While he was splashing water with one hand, Gary plucked at Dan's bra strap with his other hand and let it snap onto his back. Dan, surprised, wriggled out of his grasp and moved away.

"That's his favourite trick," Gloria said. "What he gets out of it - other than annoying the girl he is doing it to - I've no idea."

Sarah was suddenly alert. "He's not trying to get her bra off, is he?"

"Oh no. I don't think so. I think it is something he did to girls when he was at school. He thought it was a huge joke and still does, the moron."

The water fight seemed to be over. Gary had climbed onto a floating mattress and lay on it like a beached whale, while Dan and James swam slowly, side by side, at the deep end of the pool, talking quietly.

Sarah looked at Gloria. "Can I ask you something?"

"Of course."

"Why do you stay with him?"

Gloria laughed cynically. "Why do you think? All this…" she waved an arm about her. "I can't do poor any more, Sarah, and that is what I would be if I left him. Anyway…"

There was another commotion in the pool. Dan and James had swum under Gary's mattress and tipped him off. As Dan turned his back, Gary made another grab for his bra strap and when he let it go it made a loud crack that both Gloria and Sarah could hear. "Gotcha!" he shouted gleefully.

"Oh for Christ's sake!" Gloria muttered.

Dan had clearly had enough. He clambered out of the pool, picked up his towel and stalked back to the shepherd's hut. He did not turn round when James shouted "Daisy, are you OK?"

Gloria stood up. "What happened? Is Daisy all right."

"I think so," James replied. "Dad was doing his famous bra-snapping trick and I don't think she liked it."

"It was only a bit of fun," Gary said sheepishly.

"When are you bloody well going to grow up?" Gloria snarled at her husband.

A few minutes later, Dan emerged from the shepherd's hut fully dressed, but with his wet hair hanging loose. Gary, now out of the pool, waddled across to him and apologised if he had upset him. Dan said it was OK and reluctantly submitted to a hug and as they walked back together to where the women were sitting Sarah whispered to Gloria "Why is Gary walking in that strange way?".

"The bastard's got an erection," she whispered back.

* * * * *

Driving home - Sarah decided she had sobered up enough - she asked Dan if

James' father had spoiled the visit. No not really, he replied. He did not like him very much, but then James did not like him either.

"I was just wondering," Sarah said, "because James' mother asked me if I would allow you join them on their annual summer holiday this year."

Dan's heart skipped a beat. The thought of spending a holiday with James - even if his horrible father was around - made his head spin.

"Well would you?" he asked.

"If you'd like to do that, yes."

"Oh my God, when?"

"I think they leave in about six weeks."

"Where?"

"Apparently they've got a holiday home in St Lucia."

"Oh my God, St Lucia. Oh my God."

As soon as they got home, Dan raced up to his room, slammed the door and called James. "Is it true?" he demanded when James picked up.

"Is what true?" James asked, pretending ignorance.

"That I can come on holiday with you?"

"If your Mum agrees, yes."

"Oh my God, of course she agrees."

"Great, then you're on. You'll love it there. But you realise my Dad will be there the whole time?"

"Yeah, but you'll be there too and we can be together. That's all I care about."

"Shall I tell you something else exciting?"

"What could be more exciting than being with you every day?"

"It won't just be every day."

"What do you mean?"

"I overheard my parents discussing the arrangements. You'll never guess.'

"No, tell me."

"They're going to let us share a bedroom."

Dan thought he was going to faint.

"Oh…. my…. God…." he said at last.

CHAPTER 15

Although Dan and James spent almost every weekend together and had spent hours snogging in James' car with the windows steamed up, there had never been a real opportunity for them to have proper sex without the risk of being discovered. James knew dozens of discreet parking places on the Downs where they could stick their tongues down each other's throats and engage in what they called "MM" - their secret code for mutual masturbation - but sex remained off the agenda. Firstly the back of James' Mini was too small for such activity and the thought of doing it outside on the ground held little attraction, not least for fear that a walker would almost inevitably turn up at the wrong moment.

They often took walks on Beachy Head and would surreptitiously look around for hidden places off the beaten track that might be safe, but the truth was that nowhere was safe. It seemed the only way to relieve their aching genitals was by jerking each other off and with that they had to be satisfied, although one dark night on Brighton beach, when James was certain no one was around, he lifted Dan's skirt, pulled down his tights, pushed his knickers to one side, fished out his penis and put it in his mouth. Dan shivering like mad in anticipation, exploded almost immediately. It was the first time James had given anyone a blow job and it was somehow rather unsatisfactory, leaving him with an unpleasant salty taste in his mouth.

	They talked occasionally about renting a room in a hotel - James had his own credit card - but their only attempt fell at the first hurdle and they never tried it again. James wanted somewhere nice, so he chose the Grand, the posh wedding cake hotel on Brighton's seafront. In preparation, they both dressed up for the occasion. James wore a suit and and Dan wore a new dress that James had bought him the previous day, tights and high heels. Both were in a high state of anxiety. Dan had a tube of KY Jelly in his handbag, purchased that morning at the self-service till in Boots.

The doorman tipped his bowler hat as they went through the swing doors. Dan settled himself on a red plush settee trying to appear calm while James nervously approached reception. One of the receptionists, a silver-haired distinguished gentleman with a carnation in his buttonhole, smiled and said "Good afternoon sir. How can I help?"

James swallowed and asked if there were rooms available. "Yes, of course sir," the receptionist said, moving to a computer keyboard. "How long will you be staying with us?"

Without thinking, James said "Just the afternoon." He immediately realised his mistake and could have kicked himself.

The receptionist's eyebrows shot up. "Oh," he said stiffly, "I'm sorry sir, but I am afraid the Grand does not rent rooms by the hour."

By then all the other reception staff were staring at James. Bright red in the face, he mumbled "Yes, no, er, yes. Thank you. Of course…"

The receptionist leaned across the counter and beckoned James closer. "If I might offer a word of advice, sir. You would be advised to have luggage - at least an overnight bag - next time you want to book a room. Respectable hotels don't like clients without luggage."

James, who only wanted to leave, nodded, but the receptionist was not quite finished. He inclined his head towards Dan, who was staring uneasily in their direction, and whispered "I'm sorry to disappoint your delightful young lady friend."

"Thank you," James responded, absurdly. He wanted to shout at Dan "Let's get out of here," but he crossed the vast length carpet - at least it seemed vast - to where Dan was sitting, convinced that every eye was on him. "Is something wrong?" Dan asked.

"Sort of," James said, "let's go."

He reached out for Dan's hand and they walked out with as much dignity as they could muster, which was not much. Outside, in the forecourt of the Grand, when James explained what had happened Dan could not stop laughing. Once he had got over his embarrassment, James joined him. They stood giggling and holding each other up while the bemused doorman looked on. When they had recovered their composure, James suggested trying the Hilton Metropole next door - "This time I'll try and remember to say we are staying the night" he promised - but Dan shook his head. "No," he said, "Let's wait now until we get to St Lucia."

In truth, Dan was more relieved than disappointed that he had not lost his virginity. He had seen anal intercourse on gay porn websites hundreds of times and it never seemed as if the recipients were enjoying it very much; they were usually gritting their teeth or grimacing. He wanted to do it because he knew that was what James wanted, but he was worried it was going to hurt and so he was happy to wait.

The barely credible news that they were going to be allowed to share a bedroom in St Lucia had come as a surprise to both of them. Apparently it had been discussed and agreed after they had gone out for a walk the day Dan and his mother had visited James' house for the first time. Once Sarah had said that she thought it was a lovely idea for Daisy to join them in St Lucia the conversation turned to sleeping arrangements and it was

Gloria who had suggested they should sleep together. "Let's face it," she had said, "they're obviously very keen on each other and they are going to be sneaking into each other's rooms. I would much rather we all be honest and open about it.."

"Yes," Sarah had said doubtfully. "But Daisy *is* only sixteen."

Gary snorted. "When roses are red they're ready for plucking. When girls are sixteen they're ready for…"

"Thank you Gary," Gloria snapped, interrupting him. She rolled her eyes and said to Sarah "You can always really on my husband to make a mature contribution to the debate."

Sarah laughed. Wanting to be polite she asked Gary what he thought. "I lost my virginity long before I was 16," he replied. "Yeah, let 'em sleep together. The sooner they learn about sex the better."

And so it was decided. Both mothers privately admitted to a frisson of pleasure from their secret knowledge and from the fact that a notorious homophobe was unconsciously facilitating an homosexual relationship.

The Mitchisons were due to leave for St Lucia at the start of the summer holidays; Dan was to fly out a week later, a few days after his 17th birthday. As the day of his departure grew near, he became more and more anxious. He would not only be travelling alone for the first time, but he would also be travelling as a girl for the first time.

Sarah had organised a new passport for him as "Daisy Walter" with "F" in the sex box and a photo with his hair pinned up, full make-up and earrings. It was, she discovered, surprisingly easy. All she had to do was supply a letter from his GP confirming that his gender change was "intended to be permanent". She photocopied the heading of a genuine letter from their GP's surgery onto a blank sheet of paper and used it to print the requisite letter.

Despite his new passport Dan was still tormented by fears that something would go wrong and his imagination ran riot every night when he was trying to get to sleep and then, when sleep finally came, he would be troubled by dreams, almost always about being publicly exposed. In one he was standing on a chair wearing a dress but no knickers in room crowded with strangers and James' father appeared and slowly lifted his skirt and boomed "See, I told you! He's not a girl at all. He's just a sissy boy" and then everyone in the room began laughing and chanting "Sissy! Sissy! Sissy!" and Dan, unable to hold on any longer, began urinating. He woke up to discover he had wet his bed.

Sarah did her best to reassure him, as did his friends at school, who were almost all girls - boys tended to ignore him. Even Toby, his surly younger brother, told him not to worry; everyone knew he was really a girl. "I don't think you were ever a proper boy," he said. "Is that supposed to be a compliment?" Dan asked. "No!" his brother grunted.

Dan told no one except April, his best girl friend, about the sleeping arrangements in St Lucia. They had had a rift when Dan left the party without her on the night he had met James. "Girl friends are supposed to stay together and look after each other when they go out together," she had said the following day. "Maybe you've still got to learn things about being a girl." "I couldn't find you," he had protested. "I thought you had left *me*." Dan never admitted he had seen her having sex at the back of the club, but he was not surprised by her blasé reaction when he told her he would be sharing a bed with James. "Great," she said. "At least you don't have to worry about getting pregnant."

"No," he replied, "but I've never, er, you know…"

"What had it up the bum?"

Dan felt himself blushing. He shook his head.

"Oh, don't worry," she continued breezily, "you'll soon get used to it. It's a bit uncomfortable at first, but then…"

Dan was quite shocked. "You mean you've done it?"

"Oh yeah. Some blokes prefer it. Don't ask me why."

April offered to let Dan borrow anything he wanted - she had lots of summer dresses and beachwear - but he declined. His mother was determined to make sure he had everything he needed - and more - and took him shopping almost every day. "I want you to be the best-dressed girl in St Lucia," she said more than once, "and I want the Mitchisons to be proud of their son's elegant girl friend."

On the day before his departure he had another session with Alison at the salon to get his hair re-tinted, eyebrows threaded, eyelashes extended, legs waxed, a pedicure and manicure. It was odd: the girls seemed as excited as he was at the prospect of his trip. "It's so romantic," an intern called Kelly said dreamily, "jetting off to the Caribbean to meet your lover…"

"Well," Dan protested, "he's not really my lover. Just my boy friend."

"Well he will be your lover, won't he? It's like a movie. Boy becomes girl, girl meets boy… Is he tall, dark and handsome?"

"Well, he's tall and handsome but not dark," Dan said, pleased, despite himself, by the attention.

That evening, Sarah took him out to dinner to Donatello, his favourite Italian restaurant. Toby refused to join them. He wore one of several new dresses his mother had bought him for the holiday, but for which he did not have enough room in his suitcase. Sarah was proud of her beautiful boy/girl, proud that he had transitioned so effortlessly, proud of the admiring glances he got from men everywhere he went. She wanted to show him off to the world; wanted to shout "This is my son. I have made him into a girl. Isn't she beautiful?"

During the meal they talked a lot about the Mitchisons and about James. Sarah imagined Dan had already had sex with James, but there was no way she could find out without asking him direct and she was not about to do that. She could sense that Dan was still troubled by the risk of exposure and she was not surprised when, while they were waiting for coffee, he suddenly said: "Mum, what am I going to do if he finds out?"

"Who?"

"James' father. What if he finds out?" There was no need for Dan to clarify what he was saying.

"He won't," Sarah said firmly.

Dan was a silent for a moment. "But what if he does?" he insisted.

Sarah sighed. "Daisy, you've got to try and relax. Unless Mr Mitchison sees you naked - and that's not going to happen, is it? - he will never, ever, find out the truth about you. You're a girl. You look like a girl. You act like a girl. You'll probably have to put up with James' father ogling you, but that's all."

There was another pause, then Dan said "Mrs Mitchison knows, doesn't she?"

"Yes. She also knows that James is gay and so she understands the attraction you have for each other. She will never let either secret out, you can be sure of that."

Dan thought about it. "I suppose so," he mumbled doubtfully.

Sarah thought she would call his bluff. "Daisy", she said, "you do want to go on this holiday, don't you?"

"Of course I do!"

"Well then, cheer up and stop fretting. Everything will be fine and I'm sure you will have a wonderful time. Let's go."

As they got up from their table, two waiters stepped forward to help. "Thank you beautiful ladies." one of them said, "please come again." Dan giggled.

To his surprise, he slept soundly that night. He was woken at five o'clock by the alarm on his phone and spent the best part of an hour getting ready after he had had a shower. He had discussed with his mother what he was going to wear for the journey and had laid out his clothes the night before - a dark green A-line mini skirt with a striped top and ankle boots. He had intended to wear skinny jeans, but his mother dissuaded him with the sensible argument that it was much easier going to the loo on a plane wearing a skirt.

"Are you sure you have got everything?" his mother asked before they left the house. Dan checked his handbag - for the umpteenth time - for his new passport and boarding pass and nodded. Sarah thought he looked very pale. "Are you all right?" she asked. Again he nodded. "OK, let's go."

On their way to Gatwick in his mother's car Dan found that his excitement at soon seeing James was beginning to overcome his nerves and he suggested to his mother that she should simply drop him off at the terminal rather than go to the bother of parking and accompanying him to the check-in desk. "Are you sure you will be all right?" she asked.

Dan groaned. "Mum, will you stop asking me if I will be all right? Off course I will."

"Well, if you're sure?"

"I am."

Sarah was quite relieved. It would be easier saying goodbye to him outside the terminal, rather than watch him disappear into security. He was only going away for two weeks, but she knew she would miss him terribly. She cast a sidelong glance at him in the car and once again marvelled at his transition. Even when she had first suggested buying him a girl's wardrobe, she never dared to hope he would end up living happily as a girl and being accepted as a girl. She counted herself extraordinarily lucky, not for the first time.

In recent weeks she had become close friends with Gloria Mitchison and learned more about the family. Gloria had warned Sarah that Gary would almost certainly try to hit on Daisy, but she personally would make sure he did not succeed. "Don't worry," she said, "I'll make sure Daisy is never alone with the bastard."

Sarah was amazed by the range of rude epithets Gloria used to describe her husband.

As they pulled up at the "Drop-Off Only" space outside the Terminal, Sarah managed to resist the temptation to ask Dan if he was sure he did not want her to go in with him. She got out of the car and helped Dan retrieve his wheelie suitcase from the back, then there was a moment of embarrassed silence before they said goodbye. "Have a great time, sweetheart," Sarah said, giving him a hug. "Be careful and give my love to James."

"I will," Dan said. "Thanks for the lift. See you in two weeks. 'Bye."

Sarah watched him as he trundled his suitcase towards the double doors that led to Departures. She was comforted by the fact that he looked like any teenage girl, although prettier and better dressed than most, going off on holiday. His skirt was very short but he had learned how to handle it and protect his modesty, so she was not worried about that. At the doors he turned and waved to his mother. Sarah blew him a kiss and he disappeared into the Terminal.

Dan checked his watch. Two and a half hours before his British Airways flight was due to depart. (The Mitchisons had insisted on paying his fare and booking him a Club Class seat. "We always travel Club," Gary Mitchison had boasted, "why shouldn't you?") At the check-in desk he suffered a moment of panic when he presented his passport and the young man behind the desk seemed to take a long time examining it. He almost expected him to look up and say "This passport's a fake. It says you're a girl!" Instead, he looked up and smiled and said "Do you know the way to the lounge, Miss?"

Safely through security (he had had nightmares about the X-ray machine bleeping and being taken to one side and asked to undress) he began to enjoy his independence. It was rare these days for him to be out and about alone. He wandered aimlessly around the shops for a little while, treated himself to a bra and knicker set in Victoria's Secret and a new lipstick in Boots, then made his way to the Club lounge. He was amazed by the luxury of it all - the sofas and armchairs, the food and the drink. "Is it all free?" he asked a waiter. "Of course, Miss," he replied. "Can I get you something?"

Dan settled into an armchair, crossed his legs, pulled down the hem of his skirt and took his phone out of his handbag. He was hoping for a message from James, but then he remembered it was five o'clock in the morning in St Lucia. He tapped out a new message: "ON MY WAY. DONT 4GET 2 MEET ME. LONGING 2 C U." and clicked on Send.

Before his flight was called he used the Ladies and checked his make-up (the days when he was nervous about entering a Ladies' lavatory were long gone). He could feel his excitement rising as he headed towards the departure gate, clutching his passport and boarding pass, both in the name of Daisy Walter, in one hand.

"Good morning, Miss, welcome aboard," a silver-haired flight attendant said, extending a hand for his boarding pass. "Ah yes, 14A. Second aisle, turn left. Enjoy your flight."

Dan had never flown business class before. As in the lounge, he was amazed by the facilities, the seat that turned into a bed, the big television, the screen between the seats that could be raised or lowered at the touch of a button. A young male flight attendant was happy to show him how everything worked and then asked him if he would like a glass of champagne. Dan shook his head and accepted water.

For the duration of the eight hour and 45 minute flight Dan was too excited to sleep. He was relieved when, after take-off, the passenger in the adjoining seat apologised and asked if he would mind if he put up the screen between them as he had to work. Dan said not at all; he was happy not to have to make conversation. He watched two movies and played video games and made frequent visits to the loo, which he put down to excitement.

The flight landed just ten minutes late, but there was a long and frustrating wait in immigration, where only three desks were manned and the uniformed officers behind them seemed in no hurry to process the passengers. As soon as Dan was through and entered the baggage hall his phone pinged. It was a message from James: "We're outside. Hurry up. Love J."

Dan's suitcase was already on the carousel. He was about to grab it when a porter stepped in front of him and said, in a strong Caribbean accent, "No Missy, pretty girls like you should not have to carry their own luggage. Let me."

He picked up Dan's case, put it on his shoulder and said "Follow me, Missy." As they passed through the "Exit" doors into the concourse, there was a shout of "Daisy!"and James ran forward, grabbed Dan in a bear hug and swung him round. Dan, breathless, put his arms round James' neck and kissed him.

"OK, OK, do I get a kiss too?" a voice boomed from behind James. Gary Mitchison was already deeply tanned and wearing a ghastly tropical outfit, matching shorts and an unbuttoned shirt in dazzlingly bright colours, with white loafers and no socks. When James released him Dan smiled shyly and went to shake the older man's hand but Gary had other ideas, put his arms round Dan and bent forward to try and kiss him with slobbery lips. Dan grimaced, only just managed to avert his mouth and got a wet kiss on his cheek.

"Leave her alone, Dad, she's my girl friend, not yours," James said, trying to make a joke out of it. "It's an old Caribbean tradition," his father protested, "all visiting girls have to be greeted with a kiss by their hosts…" He smirked. "…Especially if they look like Daisy." He laughed out loud at his joke. "Come on. Let's get out of here."

He led the way towards the exit, followed by Dan and James, hand in hand, and the porter, still carrying Dan's suitcase on his shoulder. Dan told him he could wheel it, but he shook his head. As they stepped into the sunshine the heat and humidity hit Dan; it was, he told his mother later on the telephone, like walking into a warm bath. By the time they reached the Mitchisons' car - a white Range Rover - he could feel the sticky damp in his armpits and groin; he was grateful he was not wearing a tight skirt.

Gary Mitchison pulled out a wad of notes from his back pocket and peeled off a couple for the porter. As soon as they were in the car - Dan and James sat in the back chatting happily and tightly holding each other's hand - Gary turned on the air-conditioning full blast and within minutes Dan felt like he was sitting in a refrigerator and shivered involuntarily. "Dad," James said, "can you turn the AC down a bit? Daisy's shivering."

It took some time to get clear of the traffic around the airport in Vieux Fort, but they were soon on a winding road threading through dense rain forest with occasional glimpses of the Pitons, the island's famous twin peaks. James explained that their house was in Rodney Bay, in the north, and that the journey would take about an hour and a half. He was still talking about the island and his plans for what they were going to do, when he realised that Dan, who had rested his head on James' shoulder, was fast asleep.

He only woke when the car turned into the courtyard of a large white house with blue shutters on a bluff overlooking the ocean and Gary beeped the horn to announce their arrival. Dan gasped as he stepped out of the car and looked around. "Oh my God," he said. "What a beautiful place!" "Yes, it's all right, isn't it?" James said, hauling Dan's suitcase out of the back. "Wait until you see our room." They both suddenly blushed and Gary Mitchison leered at them. "Do you want to rush up there now?" he inquired with a snigger.

James, acutely embarrassed, snapped "Dad!"

"What?" his father said, spreading his hands innocently as if he could not understand why his question had made them uncomfortable.

The situation was saved when the front door opened and Mrs Mitchison came out, smiling broadly. "Daisy," she said. "You've arrived. Welcome. How was your journey?"

She embraced Dan and kissed him on both cheeks. "Fine, thank you, Mrs Mitchison…" Dan began.

"Gloria, please."

"Sorry, Gloria… everything was fine. I've never travelled business class before."

"And I've never travelled in anything other than business class," Gary boomed and they all laughed politely.

Gloria immediately took charge. "Gary, why don't you take Daisy's suitcase up to her room? James you can show Daisy around, then I suggest that you, Daisy, have a shower and put on a swimsuit and come and relax by the pool. You're obviously tired…"

"I'm too excited to be tired," Dan said.

"Yes, I'll bet you are," Gary mumbled under his breath, but loud enough for everyone to hear.

Gloria fixed her husband with a poisonous glare which clearly warned him to say no more. He obviously got the message, sulkily grabbed the handle of Dan's suitcase and began wheeling it across the courtyard towards the house.

They all stood watching him for a moment. When he was out of earshot, James whispered "I'm sorry about my father. He's a pig." Dan was surprised he would be so outspoken about his father in front of his mother, but Gloria said nothing. James waited until his father had disappeared into the house before he said "OK, Daisy, time for the guided tour."

"See you later Daisy," Gloria said, "take your time." As they went off hand in hand she wondered once again how it was that this wondrous boy/girl had entered their lives and saved her son from being pilloried by his father. Just so long as her husband never discovered the secret, all would be well.

James took Dan round to the back of the house where there was an infinity pool and a large terrace with sun loungers and pointed out the path that led down to the beach. "We'll go down there later," he promised. Inside, Dan marvelled at the huge sitting room with white sofas and sliding glass doors opening onto the terrace, the dining room with a long table that would seat twelve people and the kitchen, where a black maid set down her potato peeler, bobbed a curtsey to Dan (he had to stop himself from giggling) and mumbled "Welcome Miss" in a thick Caribbean accent.

Dan could hardly wait to see the room he would be sharing with James and his heart started thumping as they approached the curved staircase leading upstairs. On the landing James teased him by pointing out the doors to his parents' room and various guest rooms. "Yes, yes," Dan whispered impatiently, "but where's *our* room?"

"Right here," James replied opening the door he was leaning against. He pulled Dan through, slammed the door shut and locked it. He pushed Dan roughly against the door, pressed his lips to Dan's, stuck his tongue down his throat and reached with one hand under his skirt and into his knickers. Dan responded enthusiastically and felt his prick hardening under James' caress. "Oh my God," he muttered when their mouths disengaged, "I've been longing for this."

James, greatly hot and bothered, whispered "Let's shower together." He led Dan into an en-suite bathroom with a large walk-in shower and began to undress him. When Dan was down to his bra and knickers James reached behind his back to unhook his bra and gasped with surprise as the bra fell away. "Oh my God," he said, "you've got little boobs." Dan, embarrassed, tried to cover his chest with his hands and arms. As James pulled down his knickers he realised it was the first time James had seen him naked.

James quickly stripped off his own clothes and then, both with bouncing boners, they stepped into the shower and lathered each other down, paying particular attention to each other's genital areas. "I'm going to have to get rid of this," Dan said, waving his prick, "if I'm going to put on a swimming costume." "No problem," James spluttered, getting down on his knees.

By the time they emerged onto the terrace, both with pink complexions and wet hair, it was pretty obvious what they had been doing but Gloria had warned her husband not to make smutty remarks that might embarrass their guest, so Gary held his tongue and restricted himself to complimenting Dan's black bikini, although Gloria noted, with disgust, he was unable to stop himself licking his lips at the sight of what he thought was a teenage girl in a bikini.

James said he wanted to show Daisy the beach before it got too dark. "We'll be back in time for supper," he said. Both his parents watched them as they disappeared down the path leading to the beach. They sat in silence for some time nursing their drinks - a gin for her and a bourbon for him - watching the sunset and a yacht drop its sails as it prepared to enter Rodney Bay marina.

Gary took a swig of bourbon and suddenly asked "Do you think there is anything strange about Daisy?"

Gloria almost choked on her drink. Trying to remain calm, she said "No. What do you mean?" She felt a vein throbbing in her forehead.

"Well what is she? Sixteen, seventeen?"

"Seventeen."

"I mean, at seventeen shouldn't she have bigger tits?" He made a cupping gesture with each hand on his chest.

Gloria was almost light-headed with relief. "Gary," she said, "some girls have big tits and some girls have little tits. Daisy is obviously the latter."

Gary was silent for several minutes while he considered this, then he said "I can't see the attraction of small tits. I like big knockers, the bigger the better."

"Yes, Gary, I'm sure you do. Why don't you get me another drink?"

She badly needed another drink.

CHAPTER 16

Lying in each other's arms on the beach in the gathering dusk with the lisp of the ocean within earshot, James whispered in Dan's ear "You know we could do it here, right here, right now. There's no one around."

"No, we couldn't," Dan said firmly.

"Why not?"

"How many reasons do you want? Firstly, your Dad could come down at any minute and if he could see what we were doing he might just guess that I'm not a girl and I'd be on the first plane home. Secondly, I don't want to do it for the first time in the open when there's a nice bed waiting for us up in the house. Thirdly…

"OK, OK… I get it. But you needn't worry about my Dad. He's usually three parts pissed by this time in the evening and he never comes down to the beach in the dark."

"Even so…" Dan said. "I'll tell you what I'll do, you naughty boy. I'll give you a BJ to keep you going."

"Now you're talking," James said. He pulled down his swimming trunks and his penis sprang out, erect, immediately. Dan laughed. "Oh you naughty, naughty boy," he whispered as he leaned over and opened his mouth.

* * * * *

When they got back to the house they found an al fresco supper of cold meats, salad, cheese and tropical fruits had been laid out on a table on the terrace. Gary Mitchison seemed to be asleep, but Gloria got up from her lounger as they approached. "Hello you two," she said. "What did you think of the beach, Daisy? Lovely, isn't it?"

Dan smiled and nodded. "Awesome."

"Ready for something to eat?"

"Yes please, but can I change out of my bikini first?"

Gloria laughed. "Of course you can my dear, we'll wait for you. Take your time. Go with her James and show her where everything is. And put on a T-shirt while you are at it."

"OK Mum."

Up in their room Dan rummaged through his suitcase for a dress and underwear and then, suddenly shy, went into the bathroom to change. It was while he was doing his make-up at the mirror over the basin that he began to feel overwhelmed by fatigue. People had told him about jet lag but it was the first time he had experienced it; he calculated he had been up and about for nearly 20 hours and he saw in the mirror, as he was pinning up his hair, that he had the bags under his eyes to prove it.

"You look nice," James said when he emerged from the bathroom.

"Thank you," Dan replied. "But I feel like crap; I'm knackered."

"Yeah, it's the same for everyone when they first arrive, but you'll be fine tomorrow."

Dan managed to stay awake over supper but as soon as the meal was over he asked his hosts if he could be excused. "If I don't get to bed soon I think I'm going to fall over," he said. The Mitchisons were sympathetic and wished him a good night's sleep.

As he got up from the table James also pushed back his chair and said "I'll come with you Daisy."

"Ooh, I wonder why," Gary Mitchison muttered audibly with a smirk.

James pretended not to have heard him. "Goodnight Mum," he said, ignoring his father.

"Don't I get a goodnight too?" Gary whined as they headed for the stairs.

Once they were inside their bedroom James locked the door and turned to Dan, who was already unzipping his dress. "Are you going to be too tired?" he asked.

Dan stepped out of his dress. "I'm sorry James, I know what you want and I know how long you have waited for this, but I just can't do it tonight. I'm really sorry…"

"That's OK," James said, struggling to hide his disappointment. "I understand. I'll just go and jerk off in the bathroom… "Don't be mad at me…" Dan protested.

"I'm joking, knucklehead," James said with a grin. "Why don't you use the bathroom first…"

By the time James had cleaned his teeth Dan was in bed and fast asleep under a single cotton sheet.

James clambered in alongside him and kissed him gently on the cheek, but he did not stir.

* * * * *

Dan woke at five o'clock just as the first strands of dawn light were filtering through the shutters. It took him a moment to remember where he was and then came to him in a rush. Oh my God, I'm in bed with James! In St Lucia! He turned and saw James spread out on the bed at his side, naked and snoring gently. Trying not to wake him, Dan slipped out and padded about the room in a nightdress he had put on more out of habit than modesty. James' room was enormous, furnished simply with a double bed and a sofa covered in blue canvas. Along one wall was a range of fitted cupboards and on another a bookshelf and a television.

Dan was not sure what to do, so he decided to unpack. Unzipping his suitcase seemed to make a loud rasping noise but James did not stir. He carefully opened the doors to the fitted cupboards and saw there was plenty of space for his things. It gave him curious pleasure to hang his dresses, skirts and tops alongside James' jackets, shirts and trousers. He found an empty drawer and stuffed his underwear into it.

James was still showing no signs of stirring, so Dan opened the double doors to the balcony, where there were two wicker chairs and a low table. He closed the doors behind him, lest the light disturbed James, and settled in one of the chairs. It really was, he thought, paradise. The rising sun was reflecting off the shimmering ocean, the birds were beginning to sing and the air was fresh and warm.

He could not completely relax because at the back of his mind was the certain knowledge that he could no longer put off having sex with James. It was not that he did not want to have sex; he did. But he was sure it would hurt and he was not at all sure he would enjoy it.

A few weeks ago James had bought him a dildo, something called a "Love Honey Triple Tickler", in the unmistakable shape of a large penis, coloured purple. When Dan looked at it aghast, James had insisted it was a joke, just a bit of fun, but Dan was not so sure. He felt that James might want him to try it out, to prepare himself for sex, so he did. Alone in his bedroom, with the door securely locked, he did his best to insert the "Love Honey Triple Tickler" into his anus and failed miserably, despite liberal applications of KY Jelly, which his friend April had advised him was essential for "going in the back door". He felt he might have succeeded if he had been able to pull the cheeks of his arse apart with both hands, but that left no hand available to try and push the thing in, which was a relief, really.

  As the sun finally cleared the distant horizon, Dan noticed the maid crossing the garden carrying what looked like a heavy bag of groceries. She looked up and saw him sitting on the balcony and waved. He waved back. He heard her opening and closing the kitchen door, but there was still no sound from the rest of the house so he decided to take a shower; his skin already felt clammy from the heat.

He was putting conditioner on his hair - it now stretched down to his shoulder blades - when James appeared, naked and yawning sleepily. "Can I come in with you?" he asked. Dan nodded. James stepped in to the shower, planted his mouth on Dan's, put a hand round the back of his neck and thrust his tongue into his throat. They were soon wrestling under the flow of water, their bodies wet and slippery, each with a rock-hard erection. "Shall I give you a BJ?" Dan panted.

James shook his head. "I've got a better idea. Turn round, bend forward a bit and put your hands on the tiles." Dan did not need to guess what was a going to happen.

"I don't think this is a good idea," he whispered, water streaming down his face like tears.

"Let's just try," James insisted. "It could be fun."

Very reluctantly, Dan turned round, stepped back from the shower wall and bent forward, bracing himself against the tiles with both hands. He could feel James soaping his anus but his sphincter tightened instinctively as James tried to insert a finger. "Try and relax," he said. "How can I?" Dan muttered. After a lot of soapy probing and massaging, James finally managed to insert one finger, then two, into Dan's anus. "Are you all right?" he asked. "Sort of," Dan grunted.

James put an arm round Dan's waist, removed his fingers and tried to replace them with his penis, but the harder he pushed the more tightly Den clenched his sphincter. "I'm sorry," he whispered over his shoulder, "I can't help it." He heard James groan "Oh no!" and felt the pressure on his anus ease. "What's happened?" he asked. "I've bloody come, haven't I?" James replied.

Dan wanted to laugh but he could sense James' frustration and so he kept a straight face. "Never mind, babe," he said, "we'll try again later."

James' father, bare-chested and wearing another horrible pair of baggy Hawaiian shorts, was sitting at the breakfast table with a coffee when they came downstairs. "Hello you two lovebirds," he said, "did James let you get any sleep? You wouldn't have done if I had been him. "

Dan had a habit of twiddling with his hair if he was uncomfortable or embarrassed and he was doing it now. "Leave it Dad," James warned his father, then turning to Dan he said "Don't take any notice of my father, Daisy, he can't help it."

"Oh did I embarrass you, Daisy?" Gary said with heavy sarcasm. "Come and sit on my lap and I'll make it better," he added, pushing back his chair and holding out his arms.

"Ignore him, Dais," James said. "Dais", pronounced "days" was James' diminutive for Daisy.

Dan had borrowed one of James' shirts to wear over his bikini for breakfast. Gary eyed him up and down and said "You don't have to cover up for me you know. When it's as hot as this I think you should wear as little as possible, particularly if you are a girl." He laughed loudly as if he had cracked a great joke, making his stomach, which overhung the waistband of his shorts, quiver.

Dan smiled politely. "I'm not really used to walking around in a bikini," he explained.

"You'll soon get used to it here, won't she James?" Gary said. "This place is swimsuit central."

James ignored the question. "We're thinking of going into Rodney Bay after breakfast. Is it OK if I take Mum's car?"

Gary shrugged. "If it's OK with her." Gloria appeared at that moment from the kitchen, looking cool and elegant in a silk kimono. She smiled at Dan and kissed him on both cheeks. "Everything OK?" she whispered. Dan nodded.

Over breakfast - sweet plantain hash and eggs, cooked by the maid - plans for the day were made. Gloria not only agreed to James borrowing her car that morning, she suggested he should make free use of it all the while Dan was staying with them. "It would be nice if you could show Daisy round and let her see as much of the island as possible, although…" she turned to Dan "…we hope this won't be your only visit." Dan could feel himself blushing again. Gloria laughed and said "You look so sweet when you blush," making Dan blush even more.

Gloria insisted that Dan could go into town just as he was - "We're very laid back here," she explained - but

Dan wanted to change into a dress. When he came back downstairs with smokey eyes, red lips, his hair pinned up, wearing a yellow cotton sun dress with a very short skirt and espadrilles, Gary let out a slow wolf whistle. "I think I'll come with you," he said, then, registering the dismay on his son's face, he laughed. "Only kidding."

"Let's go, Daisy," James said, taking Dan's hand. "See you all later." Gloria's car - a new Mini convertible with the hood down - was already parked in the courtyard at the front of the house. James opened the passenger door for Dan then walked round and got into the driver's seat. As he slammed the door and buckled his seat belt, he said "One day I think I am going to kill my father and no jury will convict when they learn what an asshole he is."

"Oh, he's not so bad." Dan said uncertainly.

"Yes he is. He's worse. If he ever found out about you, Dais, I can tell you our lives would not be worth living. I mean it."

Dan swallowed. "Well, we must make sure he never finds out, mustn't we?"

James nodded grimly, put the car into gear and they set off, heading for the causeway leading to Fort Rodney on Pigeon Island, from where they could get the best view of Stn Lucia. James seemed to know a lot about the history of the place. The fort was named after Admiral George Rodney, he explained, who built it in the late 18th century on a hilltop to spy on the French naval base on the neighbouring island of Martinique. In 1782 Admiral Rodney demolished the French fleet in a famous sea battle. Pigeon Island was only recently connected to St Lucia with a causeway, using soil excavated to build Rodney Bay marina…

Dan loved listening to James, loved the fact he knew so much, loved the warm wind blowing through his hair, loved looking at the lush tropical forest they were driving through and the brightly coloured birds flitting about the treetops, loved everything about his life at that moment: that he was in the Caribbean, driving with a boy who shortly, he was certain, would become his lover. He wanted to shout with exhilaration.

After wandering around Fort Rodney hand in hand and admiring the old cannons and the 360-degree view, they drove down to the marina and had a coffee on a terrace overlooking the ranks of superyachts - mainly gin palaces with the occasional classic yacht - moored side by side within the embrace of the breakwater.

"How much do you think that lot is worth?" James asked.

"I've no idea," Dan replied. "Ten million?"

"More like a billion."

"No! Will you buy me one?"

"Of course. Just choose."

Dan stood up to get a better look and found the biggest boat in the marina - a towering motor yacht that looked like a small liner with two crew members in matching uniforms swabbing the deck. James ran a hand up his leg and Dan pretended to be shocked, slapping his hand away. "That one!" he said, pointing to it.

"It's yours. OK, let's go and do some more shopping."

Rodney Bay "village" was not like any village Dan had ever seen - bustling streets, crowds of tourists, lots of hotels and restaurants and two shopping malls. James seemed to delight in shopping with Dan, taking him into dress shops and persuading him try stuff on. In a jewellers in Baywalk Shopping Mall he ignored Dan's protests that he did not want anything and bought him an expensive pair of gold hoop earrings which, at James' insistence, he wore out of the shop. Dan noticed he paid with an American Express card.

"What if your father finds out that you are buying things for me?" Dan asked.

"This card is on my mother's account," James replied, "so he never knows how much I am spending and my mother doesn't care - she loves spending his money."

From the village it was only a five-minute drive to Reduit beach, the finest, James said, on the island. They walked along the white sand and paddled in the crystal clear water. The sea looked so inviting that Dan regretted that he had changed out of his bikini - he would have loved to have plunged in.

At Spinnakers Restaurant, right on the beach, the black maitre d' greeted James effusively. "Welcome Mr James, how lovely to see you. How is your father, well I hope?"

"Yes" James said, "unfortunately."

The maitre d' paused for a moment to take in what James had said, then threw back his head in a loud guffaw.

"He thought I was joking," James said after they had been shown to a table, "but I wasn't."

After lunch - grilled lobster and a glass of chardonnay for James, and sparkling water for Dan - James leaned forward and said "My parents always take a nap in the afternoon…" he paused "… I think we should too, don't you?"

As they made eye contact, Dan could feel a stirring in his knickers. He smiled.

CHAPTER 17

Later Dan would tell his friend April that it hurt, it hurt like hell. "It was like someone sticking a red hot poker up me," he said.

They had rushed back from Spinnakers with James driving like a mad thing. No one seemed to be around when they got back to the house and so they went straight up to James' bedroom. After he had locked the door he turned to Dan and raised his eyebrows. Dan nodded and unzipped his dress as James stripped off his T-shirt, shorts and boxers.

Within minutes they were naked and in bed together under the cool sheets, both with throbbing erections. Neither of them spoke. Dan was on his back with his legs in the air as James worked on his anus with KY jelly, slipping his fingers in and out. When he tried to insert his penis he still found his entry blocked until Dan reached down with both hands and pulled the cheeks of his arse apart and suddenly James was in him. Dan gasped with the pain but tried, for James' sake, to make it seem like a gasp of passion. "Ooh," he grunted "that's lovely." James climaxed instantly and to Dan's relief, his penis shrivelled and popped out.

    They slept contentedly in each other's arms until James' father rapped on the door and called out that it was six o'clock and time they appeared downstairs. As they disengaged from each other and sleepily climbed out of bed Dan asked if he should put on the same dress so that his parents would not guess what they had been doing. James laughed. "I think they will have a fair idea of what we have been doing," he said.

They made love again when they went to bed that night and again when they woke up in the morning and again when they had a nap in the afternoon and that was how the pattern continued, day after day. On each occasion it got easier for Dan and seemingly more pleasurable for James as he was able to sustain his erection for longer, pumping in and out until a groan signalled his inevitable orgasm. Later Dan would wonder why they never reversed their positions, but it simply never occurred to him; neither, apparently, did it occur to James. Dan was always the ridden, James the enthusiastic rider. It was the way it was.

Dan's main pleasure was the obvious pleasure he was giving James and doing it the way they did he could see James' face. He never had an orgasm while James was in him and relied on BJs for his own needs. But what their sex did was make Dan feel desirable in a way he had never experienced before. He liked the hungry way

James looked at him, liked it when James took every opportunity to touch him, liked the fact that James *wanted* him, liked his ability to flirt and produce an instant bulge in James' shorts.

None of this went unnoticed by Gloria Mitchison, who could see that the two young people were becoming increasingly obsessed with each other. She was pleased, but increasingly worried that Dan's secret would come out one day and that their relationship would founder in the face of her husband's fury. She was also worried about herself. If Gary ever found out that she knew all along Daisy was a boy she doubted their marriage would survive. As far as Gary was concerned, his son had got himself a very tasty girl friend, one he would not mind fucking himself if ever got the chance, except Gloria watched him like a hawk. One morning he had lingered outside James' bedroom door and had heard from within the muffled, but unmistakeable, grunt and gasp of sexual congress. Christ, he thought, I would like a bit of that. He rushed off to a bathroom to jerk off, imagining himself to be locked between Daisy's soft thighs

    Dan and James went out sightseeing most days. (Dan had told James that he did not like the way his father looked at him as if he was about to lick his lips; it gave him the creeps, he said.) They visited the sulphur springs at Soufrière, took zip rides through the rainforest, toured around the majestic Pitons, went on boat trips and explored the island's innumerable white sand beaches. They always made a point of returning home in time for their afternoon "nap", which rarely involved sleep so much as sweaty wrestling on the bed and Dan being penetrated while lying on his back with his legs in the air.

    A few days before Dan was due to leave, James made a decision: that he would cut his holiday short and return to the UK with Dan. He announced it to his parents that evening. Gloria was not in the least surprised, but his father professed to be surprised and offended. "We always stay six weeks," he complained. "You usually say you wished we could stay longer and now you want to go home early because you want to be with Daisy. She'll still be there when you get home, you know…"

"Yeah, I know," James said, "but I'll be going off to uni soon so I want to be able to spend as much time with her as I can before then."

"Well, here's a better idea," Gary said, brightening at the thought. "Rather than you going home early, why doesn't Daisy stay longer?"

James sighed. "Because her Mum wants her to come home."

That was not strictly true. The main reason why James wanted to return early, apart from spending more time with Dan, was that there would be an empty house -

his parents' - which they could use for sex. Both of them were acutely aware that once back in England they would face the problems that existed before the holiday: that there was no safe place they could go - as James put it so delicately - to "fuck each other's brains out."

Gloria interceded on her son's behalf. "Look Gary, it's obvious they want to be together. There's no reason why we should keep James here if he wants to go back with Daisy."

No reason, Gary thought, other than that he would miss leching after this pretty teenager and fantasising about what he would do to her if he ever got the chance. "I suppose you're right," he said reluctantly.

"Thanks Dad," James said. "I'll set it up." He went upstairs to break the good news to Dan, who was upstairs changing from a swimsuit into a dress. They celebrated with a quickie before Dan had got his knickers on.

Three days later, the Mitchisons were driving Dan and James to Hewanorra airport. Gary was still whining about how there was really no need for them to be leaving early and how he had got used to having Daisy around "brightening the place up". Gloria rolled her eyes. Privately she was more than thankful that the trip had been a success and that her husband had no inkling of how he had been deceived. Her view was that the longer Daisy stayed the greater was the risk of exposure and so she was thankful to be packing them off. At airport Gloria gave Dan a long hug and whispered "Have fun in Rottingdean", which made him blush.

Settled in their Club Class seats after take-off, James leaned across to Dan and whispered "Fancy joining the mile-high club?"

Dan giggled. "In your dreams," he said.

CHAPTER 18

While Dan was in St Lucia, his brother Toby flew to New York for his annual visit to his father in New York. Usually, both boys went but with Tristram unaware of his older son's transition Sarah knew it would be impossible this year and started making vague excuses for him even before he had been invited to St Lucia.

Tristram was not pleased. In a long and bad-tempered transatlantic telephone call with his former wife, he had made it clear he was expecting both boys as usual and when Sarah had prevaricated he had demanded "Sarah, what the fuck is going on? Dan comes to see us every year. What's changed?"

Sarah's mind was racing to try and find a suitable excuse. Tristram had called unexpectedly in response to an e-mail she had sent suggesting that Dan might not be able to join his brother this year. "Well," she said, "it's just that she..."

She stopped. She could have bitten her tongue off.

Tristram jumped on her mistake. "She? Who's she?"

"Well it's um, er, sorry, I was thinking of my sister. Yes, that's right, Eve is planning a big family reunion at the time when Dan would normally be visiting you and he really wants to be there."

There was a momentary silence at the other end of the line. Finally Tristram spoke, his voice heavy with sarcasm. "You're telling me that Dan would rather attend a fucking family fucking reunion than visit his father in New York? You're not serious."

"Look Tristram, I've got to go," Sarah said. "There's someone at the door. I'll e-mail you." She cut the line before he could object.

A week later Dan was invited to join the Mitchisons in St Lucia, providing Sarah with a ready-made excuse, as she explained in an e-mail:

"Tristram, Dan may not have told you he has a serious girl friend, a very pretty girl called Daisy, whose family spends every summer at their house on St Lucia. They have invited Dan to join them this year. The dates they can manage clash with the boys' usual visit to you. Dan was very worried that you would be upset if he cancelled, but I said I was sure you would understand. He obviously wants to spend time with his girl friend and a trip to the Caribbean is an added bonus. Please don't make trouble about this. Sarah."

Tristram's reply was succinct. *"Fuck you, Sarah. It's obvious you have been trying to find a way to stop Dan visiting me and now you have succeeded. Fuck you, you bitch."*

Toby was relieved when he learned he would be travelling to New York alone. He was dreading his mother announcing that she had told their father that Dan was now Daisy and that he would have to suffer the hideous embarrassment of turning up in New York with his brother wearing a dress.

Although Sarah believed that her younger son had accepted the new family dynamic, he was still greatly troubled by what had happened and was often teased by his football mates about his boy/girl "sister". He nearly broke his mother's heart one time when Dan was in St Lucia and he asked her sadly if they would ever be "a normal family" again.

"Don't be silly," she had replied as brightly as she could manage, "we're a normal family now."

"How can we be normal," he had persisted, "when I have to pretend my brother is my sister?"

Sarah hesitated. "Sometimes things happen that are beyond our control," she said. "I know you find it difficult, but it'll get easier and easier as time goes by. I promise you."

Toby was not prepared to let the subject drop. "You know what Uncle Charlie told Archie?" (Archie was Eve and Charlie's oldest son.)

Sarah shook her head.

"He told him that he thought you wanted Dan to become a girl to replace Alice."

Sarah gasped involuntarily. "He had no right to say that," she said angrily, "and it's not true. Dan is living as Daisy because he wants to live as a girl, because he is more comfortable as a girl..."

"Yeah, but what about me?" Toby said, interrupting his mother. "I'm not more comfortable am I?"

Sarah sighed. "Please Toby," she said, "please don't let go through all this again."

Later that evening Sarah phoned her sister and when Charlie answered she lost her temper, telling him to mind his own business and stop spreading crackpot theories that she was trying to replace Alice. It was while she was still ranting at him that she suddenly realised that it was probably her brother-in-law who had questioned what she was doing with the Social Services. Who else could it have been? He was the only one to have linked Daisy with Alice.

"It was you, wasn't it?" she said suddenly.

"Was me what?" Charlie asked.

"Who reported me to the Social Services?"

Charlie hesitated. "Yes," he said softly. "I wanted..."

"I DON'T CARE WHAT YOU WANTED" Sarah shouted into her phone. "You shouldn't have done it. I've got enough on my plate without the bloody Social on my back."

"Sarah," Charlie began, "will you listen to me..." But the line had gone dead.

Sarah refused to speak to her sister for two weeks, during which time Toby left to visit his father. On the night before his departure Sarah once again emphasised to him the importance of keeping Daisy's existence secret.

Toby was worried. "He's sure to ask about Dan. What do I tell him?"

"Just tell him that he's fine and that he's sorry not to be with you."

Sarah had already explained that she had told Toby's father that Dan was in St Lucia with a girl friend. "Why did you have to tell him that Dan's so-called girl friend is called Daisy?" he complained. "Everything is getting in such a muddle."

"Yes, I suppose that was a bit stupid of me," Sarah admitted. "But we'll just have to live with it now."

They were talking in Toby's bedroom while he was packing his suitcase. After a silence he turned to his mother and asked "When are you going to tell him?"

Sarah feigned ignorance and raised her eyebrows. "Tell him what?"

"You know."

Sarah did know, but she had no idea what to say. Her sister kept nagging her to tell Tristram what was going on and warning her that the longer she left it the worse it was going to be. She knew Eve was right, but she just could not face it. Tristram was going to be mad whenever he found out and she had no idea what he might do, so she just put it off and put it off. "I'll tell him when the time is right," she would tell her sister and when Eve asked "When will that be?" she just shrugged.

* * * *

Toby was still in New York when Dan and James returned from St Lucia. Sarah met them at Gatwick airport. Dan looked marvellous when he emerged from the baggage claim hand in hand with James - his skin had acquired a golden tan, his hair, tied up in a loose bun, was bleached by the sun and he was wearing a dress she had never seen before. He threw his arms round his mother's neck and nodded enthusiastically when she asked him, needlessly, if he had had a good time. James just stood there with a big grin on his face while they talked.

On the way back to Brighton in Sarah's car Dan explained that he would not be returning home just yet as James's parents had asked them if they could "house-sit" the Mitchison's place in Rottingdean. Sarah smiled and said she understood. (She also understood that an empty house held a particular attraction for two young people with the hots for each other.) Over the next three weeks Dan only went home to drop off his laundry and collect more clean clothes.

Alone with James they had a lot of sex and fantasised about what the future held for them. James wanted to find a flat in Leeds, where he was to start at university, so that Dan could live with him when he (Dan) had finished school. They talked about getting married -

Dan wanted a big white dress - and adopting children and things they would do and places they would visit.

A cloud suddenly appeared on the sunny horizon they had created when Toby telephoned from New York with the news that his father was flying back with him. He had some business to conduct in London but planned to spend some time in Brighton because he wanted to see Dan. Sarah went into immediate panic mode. "What the hell am I going to do now?" she asked her sister.

"You're just going to have to tell him," she replied. "You can't let him turn up and discover that his son is now a girl."

"I can't do it, I really can't. There's got to be some other way."

She got Toby to discover that Tristram was returning to New York on September 10, then telephoned Gloria Mitchison in St Lucia to ask if Daisy could stay on for a few days in their Rottingdean house after they got back. Gloria agreed immediately. "She can stay as long as she likes," she said. Sarah did not explain why and Gloria chose not to ask.

Sarah then e-mailed Tristram. *"Sorry you won't be able to see Dan while you're here. He won't be back from St Lucia until Sept 12."*

"Why isn't he at school?" Tristram replied.

Sarah was pleased with her glib response. *"He's in the sixth form now. They go back a week later than the rest of the school."*

Dan was perfectly happy to stay on in Rottingdean and even happier to avoid seeing his father. They had to be a lot more circumspect about where and when they had sex after James' parents returned - James had most enjoyed ravishing Dan on his father's bed - but other than putting up with his Gary's boorish behaviour the arrangement worked well. James, who did not start at university until the end of the month, drove Dan to school each morning and picked him up every afternoon.

It worked well, that is, until one afternoon when Dan was walking out of school with a gaggle of girl friends and found his father standing on the other side of the road, opposite the school gates.

* * * * *

While he was in London Tristram had been given a couple of tickets for a Seagulls match against Manchester United. "Seagulls" was the nickname of Brighton & Hove Albion, the soccer team that Toby fervently supported. Tristram decided, on their spur of the moment, to drive down to Brighton, pick up Toby from school and take him to the match as a surprise.

Outside the school searching the emerging boys' faces for Toby, he was unaware of a girl detaching herself from a group of other girls and approaching him. She stopped a couple of metres from where he was standing but only when she spoke did he pay her any attention.

"Dad," she said. "It's me."

Tristram felt the blood rushing to his head as the realisation dawned that he was looking at his son.

"Dan?" he croaked.

Dan nodded.

"Jesus fucking Christ."

CHAPTER 19

Later, when the grief had somewhat assuaged, Tristram would admit he had handled the situation very badly. He was dumbstruck at the sight of his son dressed a a schoolgirl and by the fact that he almost failed to recognise him. He stared, uncomprehendingly, at his son, at his blond hair, tinted pink and blue, tied up in a pony tail with a ribbon, at his finely arched eyebrows, his mascara, his lipstick, the gold studs in his ears, at the bra discernible under his white blouse, at his short pleated skirt with its rolled-up waistband, at his long shapely legs in black tights and his Doc Martens.

"Dan," he muttered, "what the fuck is going on?"

Dan immediately regretted making himself known to his father. He could have slipped out, unnoticed, with his girl friends, jumped into James' car and left. But somehow he could not bring himself to pass his father by, even though he knew he would be giving him the shock of his life.

"I'm living as a girl now," he said, needlessly.

Tristram swallowed hard, trying to control his temper. He found it hard to believe the evidence of his own eyes. The last time he had seen Dan he was boy; now he was a girl.

"Jesus Christ," he repeated, shaking his head. "Dan, you're my son, what do you think you are doing pretending to be a girl?"

"It's just the way it is, Dad."

"What the fuck is that supposed to mean?"

Dan could see that his father's anger was building. "Look, Dad," he said. "I've got to go. You need to talk to Mum. 'Bye."

He turned and ran in the direction of James, who was standing by his car watching what was going on and wondering if he should intercede. "Let's go," Dan said as he jumped in.

"Who was that?" James's asked when he got into the driving seat.

"My Dad."

"Wow. Did he know about you?"

"No."

"Wow."

* * * * *

Tristram watched him leave and thought he might be going mad. Was that girl really his son? And did he see her kiss that boy waiting by the car? He forgot about the soccer game and forgot he was waiting for Toby, got into his rental car and drove directly to Sarah's salon in a rage. It was clear that Sarah was expecting him - Dan had telephoned to warn her from James' car - because she expressed no surprise when he burst through the front door.

"What the fuck do you think you are doing?" he shouted before the door had shut behind him. All the girls in the salon turned to look at him as Sarah, very calm, said "Hello Tristram. Please don't shout at me. Why don't we discuss this in the office?"

She led the way into the back room and closed the door behind them. Hoping to diffuse his anger she immediately apologised. "I'm sorry, Tristram. I know I should have told you what was going on but it has been so difficult these past few months..."

But Tristram was not to be deflected. "I don't want your fucking apologies, I just want to know why my son is dressing like a fucking girl. You're obviously going along with it and so you're responsible. This is going to stop and it's going to stop right now. I want my son back, do you understand?"

"Please Tristram," Sarah pleaded, "pleased let me try and explain. Dan is suffering from a condition called gender dysphoria..."

Sarah had often thought about how she would break the news to her ex-husband and so she was ready with a plausible account of how Dan had become Daisy which minimised her own role and omitted any reference to the encouragement she had given him.

Tristram was not in the least mollified. "I don't give a fuck about all this dysphoria psycho-babble shit. You should have consulted me when this started and it could have been nipped in the bud. Daisy! Christ, Sarah, what were you thinking of? What kind of mother do you think you are?"

It was Sarah's turn to lose her temper. "Don't start blaming me, you bastard. I may not be the best mother in the world but I'm a better mother than you ever were a father.."

The argument continued with raised voices that could clearly be heard by everyone in the salon. It ended with Tristram storming out, red-faced and furious, shouting about boys being boys. When Sarah emerged from her office it was obvious to everyone that she had been crying. "That was my ex-husband," she said with a wan smile. "But you probably guessed."

Tristram spend the next hour in the Painter's Arms, a pub at the end of the street, downing double whiskies. He telephoned Dan three times and left a message each time, but he did not call back. He was quite drunk by the time he showed up on the doorstep at Eve and Charlie's house and knocked on the door. Charlie opened it and his eyes widened when he saw who it was. "Tris, this is a surprise. Come in."

"Why didn't you tell me?" Tristram demanded without moving. "Why didn't you fucking tell me?"

Charlie did not need to know what he was talking about. "Come in, Tris. We need to talk."

Tristram stumbled as he crossed the threshold and grabbed Charlie to stop himself falling. "Sorry, mate, I've had a few," he explained.

"Yeah," Charlie replied, "who could blame you?"

Charlie was glad his wife and sons were out of the house so that he could talk to Tristram uninterrupted. In the sitting room he poured them both drinks and told him the whole story from the moment that Sarah first mentioned Dan's cross-dressing to the present day and how Sarah had made them promise not to reveal to him what was happening. "She kept saying she would tell you when the time was right, but I suppose she never got to that point. I'm so sorry, Tris. I kept telling her that as Dan's father you had the right to know, but she would not listen to me."

Tristram brooded over what he had learned. "Sarah's been driving this, hasn't she?" he asked suddenly.

Charlie hesitated, then nodded. "You know what I think?" he asked.

Tristram shook his head.

"I think that by encouraging Dan to be a girl she is trying to replace Alice."

Tristram's eyes widened. "Of course! That's it! I always suspected she was mad, now I know. She's screwing up Dan's life, she's got to be stopped."

Charlie, alarmed by his reaction, counselled caution. "What's been done to Dan can't be undone overnight," he warned. "He's been living as a girl for some time now. You can't expect him to suddenly revert to being a boy overnight."

"Look Charlie," Tristram said angrily. "I want my fucking son back and I'll do whatever it takes to get him back."

Later, when Charlie was recounting their conversation to his wife after Tristram had left, she looked worried. "He'll do something stupid," she predicted. "You know what he's like. He's a hothead."

* * * * *

Early next morning Tristram parked his rental car down the street from Sarah's house at a point where he could see whoever was leaving. Dan had still not responded to any of the messages he had left on his phone and so he planned to intercept him on his way to school. Shortly before 8 o'clock he saw Toby leave the house; half an hour later he was followed by Sarah. There was no sign of Dan.

He waited another 30 minutes just to be sure, then drove to Downs Comprehensive school. There was no security on the door and so he walked in and buttonholed a passing student for directions to the headmaster's office. The secretary shook her head when he said he needed to see the headmaster urgently. "I'm afraid you will have to make an appointment. Doctor Horsfall is extremely busy…"

"I am sure he is," Tristram interrupted her. "Me too. I'm just here for a few days from New York. I want you to go in there and tell him that unless I get to see him right now I am going to sue this school and him personally for facilitating and encouraging my son to deny his birth gender."

"Oh, are you Daisy Walter's father?"

Tristram rolled his eyes. "No, I'm Dan Walter's father."

The secretary had never approved of all this nonsense about young people choosing their gender and welcomed any trouble her visitor might cause. "I'll see what I can do," she said, standing up from her desk, knocking softly on the headmaster's door and disappearing inside in response to a muffled "Come in".

A few minutes later she emerged and, holding the door open, said "Doctor Horsfall will see you now."

As Tristram marched in, the headmaster stood up, smiled and held out his hand. Tristram ignored it and launched into a furious tirade about the school's "ludicrous" uniform policy and his anger that his son was being allowed to attend school in a skirt.

Eventually Horsfall held up his hand to try and get a word in. "May I ask you, Mr Walter, why you have changed your mind?"

It was a question that stopped Tristram in his tracks. "Pardon?"

"I asked why you had changed your mind."

"Changed my mind about what?"

"About allowing your son to come to school in a girl's uniform."

"I never agreed to that!" Tristram protested. "The first I knew about it was when I saw him leaving school yesterday afternoon."

"Please just wait a moment," he said to Tristram.

Horsfall pushed a button on the intercom on his desk and said "Miss Lewis, can you bring me the file on Dan/Daisy Walter?"

Miss Lewis bustled in carrying a thin brown cardboard folder which she handed to the headmaster. "Thank you, Miss Lewis," he said, "that will be all."

As she left the room, Horsfall sat down at his desk, opened the file and extracted a piece of paper, which he handed to Tristram. "This is the letter, signed by both you and your former wife, explaining that your son is suffering from gender dysphoria and authorising us to allow him to attend school in a skirt uniform."

Tristram took the letter, scanned it briefly and looked up at the headmaster. "I have never seen this in my life and that is not my signature," he said. "My former wife never discussed this with me. If she had have done, I would never have approved."

"Are you suggesting she forged your signature?" the headmaster asked.

"No, I'm not suggesting it. I'm telling you that is what she has done. She hasn't even tried to make it look like my signature. My former wife has no scruples. I believe she is behind my son's so-called gender confusion and that she is facilitating and encouraging him to change his gender in a pathetic attempt to replace our daughter, Alice, who was killed in a road accident several years ago."

Doctor Horsfall grimaced. He could see his second interview at Good Morning Britain disappearing before his eyes. "Oh dear," he said. "This complicates everything. We certainly cannot allow your son to continue at school as a girl without your permission. Do you think it would be an idea if you talked to him?"

"I think that would be an excellent idea," Tristram said.

"I'll ask Miss Lewis to fetch him."

CHAPTER 20

When Dan was called from his classroom to see the headmaster, he had a good idea what was afoot and so he was not too surprised to find his father sitting in an armchair in Donkeydrop's study. He saw his father look him up and down with disapproval, as if he did not expect to find him wearing make-up and dressed as a schoolgirl. "Hello Dad," he said.

"Hello son," Tristram replied. The male noun sounded hollow even to him, given his son's appearance.

Donkeydrop initially took charge. "Daisy, I am very sorry to tell you that the school made a mistake in believing that your father supported your desire to attend in a skirt uniform. He has made it very clear this morning that he did not do so and without his support I am afraid we cannot allow you to continue…"

Dan's mouth dropped open. "You mean I've got to go back to coming to school as a boy?"

"I'm afraid so," the headmaster replied. "I'm going to leave you here to chat things over with your father in private. Perhaps together you can sort things out." Horsfall turned to Tristram. "Please let me know if you need anything," he said, before he walked out and closed the door behind him.

"Why don't you sit down?" Tristram suggested. A wave of irritation swept over him as he watched his son sit down *exactly* as a girl would, tucking his skirt under his bottom, adjusting the hem and pressing his legs, in black tights, closely together.

They stared at each for a moment in silence, before Dan said bitterly "Thank you for ruining my life."

"No, Dan…"

"My name's Daisy."

Tristram sighed. "No, it's not, it's Dan, and I'm not ruining your life. Your mother is doing that job, very successfully and single-handedly. She never spoke to me about all this, not once, never hinted about what was going on and she forged my signature on a letter saying I supported the idea of you coming to school in a skirt when she knew full well that I would never, never agree to such a thing."

"What's it got to do with you anyway?" Dan demanded.

"Dan, I'm your father. I may not be a very good father and I may live thousands of miles away, but I am still your father and nothing can change that. You're my son, you'll always be my son and I don't want you to grow up as a freak."

"I'm not a freak!"

"No? You're a boy pretending to be a girl - that's pretty freakish in my book."

"Dad, you really don't understand, do you? Life is very different now to when you were my age. Gender is not important any more. Boys can choose to be girls and girls can choose to be boys. No one cares. I am happy and comfortable wearing a dress or wearing a skirt to school. What's so wrong with that? I can pass as a girl everywhere I go. My boy friend's father has no idea I am not a girl…"

"Your boy friend?"

Dan laughed scornfully. "Oh yes, didn't Mum tell you I have a boy friend? I was with him and his family in St Lucia. We had a great time. They're not at all small-minded. They even let us share a bedroom…"

Tristram was beginning to lose his temper. "Spare me the details, please. I've had enough of all this. As you can't continue at school as a girl, you'll have to go back dressing as a boy…"

Dan shook his head. "Forget it Dad. There's no way I'm going back to being a boy…"

"Dan you're seventeen years old and you'll do as you're told," Tristram snapped angrily. "You're a bloody boy, not a girl, can't you understand that?"

Alarmed by his father's tone, Dan was struggling not to cry. "I want to talk to Mum," he said in a voice trembling with emotion. "Why do you think you can control my life when you obviously don't care about any of us…"

"That's not true. Do you think your mother had your best interests at heart when she started encouraging you to dress as a girl, when she took you shopping for girl's clothes? No. She was doing it for herself. And do you know why Dan?"

Dan shook his head.

"Because she wanted you to replace Alice. That's what it's all about. She wanted to turn you into a girl so she felt less bad about losing Alice."

Dan stared at him with big eyes. "I don't believe you."

"Frankly, I don't care if you believe me or not. Ask you Uncle Charlie what he thinks. It was him that told me. You've been manipulated by your mother for her own ends, Dan, and that's the sorry truth that you need to face. This cross-dressing nonsense has to stop and it has to stop right now. First of all you are going to go into the bathroom and wipe all that muck off your face, then I am going to take you into town and find a hairdresser and you are going to have your hair cut very short. No more fringes and no more pink and blue bits. Then I'm going to take you home and we're going to bundle up whatever girls' stuff you now own and we're going to take it to a charity shop and… Wait!"

Dan had leapt to his feet and run out of the room, taking Tristram completely by surprise. By the time he got out into the corridor his son had disappeared.

"Do you know where he went?" he asked the secretary.

She shook her head, then said primly "We're supposed to call her 'she'."

Tristram lost it. "That was my bloody SON who just went out through that door," he shouted at her, "and there is no way in the world I am ever going to call him 'her'. As far as I am concerned you and your school can stick your bloody gender neutral uniform policy up your arse."

The secretary sniffed, disapproval written all over her face.

* * * * *

As soon as he left the headmaster's study, Dan hurried down a corridor to the cloakrooms, collected his handbag and blazer from his locker, then ran out through a back door just as his father was checking the street outside the front door. Dan knew the area well and knew that his father was very unlikely to find him, nevertheless he kept up a brisk pace in order to put as much space as possible between him and the school. He ignored the stares of workmen on a building site - he was used to men staring at him in his short skirt - and did not react when one shouted "What's the hurry, sweetheart? You running away from school?"

He did not call James until he was seated at an upstairs table at The Trading Post, a cafe they used frequently. James was obviously surprised to hear from him in the middle of the school day because he answered "What's up?"

Hearing James' voice Dan immediately burst into tears. "My Dad…" he sobbed, "… he's messed everything up… he told Donkeydrop he didn't want me to go to school as a girl… my Mum forged his signature on a letter…"

James interrupted "Where are you now?"

"At The Trading Post."

"Stay there. I'll come and get you."

As the line disconnected a woman at an adjoining table leaned across and said "Are you all right, dear? Would you like a tissue?"

Dan nodded gratefully, accepted a tissue and dried his eyes, then called his mother. She, also, was worried to get a call from him in the middle of the school day. "Daisy," she answered, "are you all right?"

"Not really," he replied, swallowing and trying hard not to start crying again. "Dad's been to the school. He says you faked his signature on some letter. Now Donkeydrop says I can't continue at school as a girl if Dad doesn't approve. It's all a big mess. He was very mean to me and so I ran off and now I'm waiting for James…"

"Daisy," his mother interrupted. "I'm going to have to call you back. Your father has just walked into the salon."

* * * * *

Tristram strode into his ex-wife's salon, grabbed her by the wrist and bundled her into the back office grunting "You and I need to talk." The argument that followed was heated and lengthy, with both parties shouting so loudly at each other that it could be heard by staff and customers alike in the main salon. One lady found it so distasteful that she got up and left half way through her manicure.

Alison, the chief stylist, twice put her head round the door to suggest that they keep the noise down and was twice told by Tristram, furiously, to "butt out."

Tristram was enraged with his ex-wife because of

her stupidity, her selfishness and her apparent willingness to ruin the life of their son by encouraging him to pretend he was a girl. He could just about accept that Dan was probably gay, but the more he thought about it the more convinced he was that Charlie Evans was right: that it all boiled down to Sarah's difficulty to deal with the loss of Alice. Charlie was a sensible bloke: he could see what was happening.

Sarah had admitted that Dan was not living at home temporarily but had refused point blank to tell Tristram where he was. "You can't stop me seeing him!" he had shouted at her. "I'm his father. I have every right to know where he is."

"Haven't you caused enough trouble already?" she had asked. "You want to know where he is, you go find him."

"That's exactly what I intend to do," he said as he walked out

Tristram had given up hope that Dan would respond to the messages he had left on his phone, so he texted Toby and asked him to call during his lunch break. At 12.30 he called. "Hey Dad," he said. "Where are you?"

"I'm in Brighton."

Toby did not try to hide his surprise. "You are?"

"Yes. I was planning to surprise you by taking you to the Seagulls' match last night. I was waiting outside the school to meet you but your brother came out first."

"Oh." Toby did not know what else to say.

"You should have told me, Toby, what was going on. All that time we spent in New York together you never said a word…"

"I'm sorry, Dad," Toby pleaded. "I really am. I wanted to tell you, I did, but Mum had made me promise…"

"I know, Toby, understand. I'm not mad with you. But I need to sort this out and need to find Dan…"

"Is he not in school?"

"No, he's walked out." Tristram did not see any reason to give his younger son any of the details. "Toby, I know Dan is not living at home right now. If you know where he is, you need to tell me."

Toby hesitated. He thought he should probably ask his mother if it was OK, but he loved his Dad and wanted to please him.

"Toby?"

"Dan's got a friend," he began slowly. (He could not bring himself to say "boy friend".) "His parents have got a big house somewhere in Rottingdean. I think he might be staying with them."

"Are these the people Dan went to St Lucia with?"

"Yes."

"Do you know their address?"

"No, but I think their name is Mitchison."

"Thank you, Toby, you have done the right thing. I'll try and see you later on after school if everything works out."

"OK, Dad. You won't tell Mum will you?"

"No, Toby, I won't. Don't worry."

* * * *

It took Tristram no time at all to find the Mitchison house in Rottingdean. The first person he stopped in the street gave him explicit directions and he was soon sitting in his car outside the closed double gates, wondering what to do next. It was unlikely that Dan had gone back to school, he thought, so if this was the right place, he could be inside.

He could see a video intercom to one side of the gates. He stepped out of his car, walked across and pressed the buzzer. After a few seconds a gruff, impatient, male voice barked "What is it?"

"I'm sorry to bother you," Tristram said into the speaker. "My name is Tristram Walter. I'm looking for my son. I think he may be staying with you."

Gary Mitchison snorted and stared more closely at the closed circuit television screen. Who was this wanker? In Gary's eyes, anyone called Tristram must, per force, be a wanker. "No mate," he said, "you've got the wrong house. Sorry."

Tristram persisted. "I think my son was recently on holiday with you in St Lucia."

Gary started to get angry. "What the fuck are you talking about? The only person on holiday with us was my son's girl friend."

"Was her name Daisy?"

"How the fuck did you know that?"

"Because Daisy is my son. His real name is Dan."

"Oh yeah?" Gary sneered. "Listen mate, I don't know who you are or what your game is, but I can tell you

I know the difference between a boy and a girl. My son's girl friend is a girl. If you don't piss off in the next two minutes I'm going to call the police."

"Won't you let me explain…" Tristram asked.

"No I won't. Just piss off."

There was a click from the intercom. Tristram assumed that whoever he had been speaking to had replaced the handset, but he was not going to give up so easily. He pressed the buzzer again.

Gary did not give him a chance to speak. "OK, that's it. I'm calling the cops!" he shouted, before there was another click.

Tristram was not particularly worried. He could not imagine the police responding to a call about an unexpected, or unwanted, visitor. But then he was not to know that Gary Mitchison made generous donations to police charities and provided most of the booze for the local nick's Christmas party. He decided to wait in his car outside the Mitchison house in the hope of intercepting Dan when he returned, but ten minutes later a flashing blue light appeared in his rear view mirror and two uniformed officers got out.

As they approached on each side of Tristram's car, he pressed the button to wind down his window. The officer on his side leaned down, smiled and said "May I ask, sir, what you are doing?"

Tristram was not in the least intimidated by two British policemen. "No you may not," he snapped.

"It's just that we've had a report of suspicious activity in this area," he continued, ignoring Tristram's rudeness.

"And I'm suspicious, am I, sitting in my car minding my own business?"

"Well, you are sitting in a rental car outside the home of one of the wealthiest men in the neighbourhood and you won't tell us what us what you are doing. That's suspicious as far as I am concerned."

"I don't want to tell you because it's none of your business."

The policeman stood up, made a what-do-you-think face to his colleague on the other side of the car, who nodded., He leaned down again to talk to Tristram through the car window. "Well, sir, perhaps you'd like to tell us down at the station."

Tristram was incredulous. "Are you arresting me?"

"No, sir, nothing like that. We'd just like you to assist with our inquiries."

"Christ," Tristram spluttered. "I'd no idea Britain had become a police state. OK, you win. I'm off." The two officers stepped aside as he started the engine and drove away.

Gary, watching the entire exchange from an upstairs window, grinned. Who the hell was that geezer, he wondered. Tristram! What a wanker. Looking for his son, then saying his son was Daisy! What was he on? Gary had no doubt that Daisy was a girl because he'd caught a glimpse of her little boobs when she was getting dressed one morning in St Lucia and had left the door to her room slightly open. She'd shut it quickly when she realised he was outside but not before he'd got an eyeful. Lovely! But how did that bloke know her name was Daisy?

Gary was alone in the house. Gloria was in London meeting a friend for lunch and James had rushed out of the house earlier and driven off without saying where he was going. Gary was about to go downstairs but then, for no particular reason, he decided to take a look into his son's bedroom, the room he was sharing, at the moment, with his girl friend. Gloria had not told him why Daisy was staying with them and he hadn't asked.

The room was a tip - the bed was unmade and clothes and underwear were scattered everywhere. Gary picked up a pair of Daisy's knickers and sniffed them before dropping them back on the floor. He began opening random drawers, not really knowing what he was doing, or why. In one of them he found Daisy's passport, which he examined closely. It was made out in the name of Daisy Walter. Didn't that geezer at the door say his name was Walter, or Walker, or something like that? He was also saying some rubbish about Daisy being his son, yet her passport photograph clearly showed she was a girl - no way would anyone think she was a boy - and then, in the sex box just under her date of birth, there was a clear "F" for female. Didn't that settle it, Mr Tristram Wanker?

Gary suddenly had a thought and began searching the drawers methodically, one after another, reaching into the back of each one and probing with his fingers. He checked the bedside tables and the fitted wardrobes, patting the pockets of the dresses and skirts hanging there and looking into the handbags Daisy had stored under the clothes rack. He went through the bathroom cabinet particularly carefully, taking everything out and setting it to one side before putting it back.

He found two tubes of KY jelly in a bedside table, but he did not find what he was looking for. Daisy, it seemed, was a girl with no need for tampons.

* * * * *

Gary Mitchison sat on the bed and tried to order his thoughts. Up until this moment he had no real doubts that Daisy was a girl, even after the visit of Mr Tristram Bleeding Wanker. By then he had spent a lot of time with her - three weeks in St Lucia and now staying with them in Rottingdean - and it had never crossed his mind for a minute that she was not what she appeared.

But now he did not know what to think. If, God forbid, he was wrong it meant that James was.... no, he did not want to think about it.

He decided there was only one way to settle the issue and the more he thought about it the more he liked the idea. He licked his lips, tentatively, in anticipation.

CHAPTER 21

James was doing his best, not very successfully, to assure Dan that everything would be OK. Dan had burst into tears as soon as James walked into The Trading Post and had cried on his shoulder uncontrollably for several minutes while James stroked his hair and tried to soothe him. They were attracting so much embarrassing attention that James helped him up from their table and led him out into the street to where he had parked his car. When Dan began to calm down they sat talking for a long time, discussing what had happened and what options remained open to them. Dan was adamant that there was no way he was going to return to school as a boy, no matter what his father said or did.

Dan called is mother again and she, too, promised him that she would sort everything out. "Your Dad will come round," she said, trying to sound confident. "He'll have to. Obviously it was a bit of a shock when he met you outside school, but he'll get used to the idea in time, I'm sure of it." Dan remained unconvinced.

Sarah made no mention of the bitter row she had just had with his father, or the fact that he had sworn to do everything in his power, including taking legal action, to get his son back. She knew there was no possibility - not even a remote possibility - of his "coming round" and accepting Dan as a girl, but she saw no point in worrying Dan any more than he already was.

Dan and James agreed they could not go back to Rottingdean without trying to find an excuse for why Dan had left school early, so they drove to Dan's house in Kemp Town, where Dan knew they would be undisturbed - his mother was at the salon and his brother at school.

Once inside, Dan took James by the hand and led him up to his bedroom. He smiled for the first time since James had found him in tears at The Trading Post, put a finger to his lips to indicate he did not want to talk and made James sit on the bed. With James watching, transfixed, Dan shrugged off his blazer, let it fall to the floor and began unbuttoning his blouse, which joined his blazer on the floor. As he unzipped his skirt he said, with a sly smile, "Aren't you going to join me?" James laughed, leapt to his feet, tore off his T-shirt and unbuckled his belt and within seconds they were lying naked together on the bed and Dan was gasping as James plunged into him.

They stayed in bed for the next two hours, talking and making lazy love intermittently. Their intimacy made Dan feel better and more optimistic and by the time they had showered and were driving back to Rottingdean he was happier than he had been at any time since seeing his father outside his school the previous day.

As they entered the house James called out "Anyone home?" and his father appeared from the sitting room with a weird sort of smile on his face that immediately made Dan feel uneasy. "Well, if it isn't the young lovers," he said in a voice heavy with sarcasm.

James ignored him and asked if his mother was home. His father shook his head. "Something's come up. I want to talk to you both. Come in here," he said, inclining his head towards the sitting room." Dan was full of foreboding as he followed James into the room.

Gary settled himself down on one of the big sofas and took a slurp from a tumbler of whisky on a table at the end of the sofa. Dan and James stood like naughty children in the centre of the room, waiting for what was coming.

"Well, there's no point beating about the bush is there?" Gary began, almost cheerfully. "Daisy, I'd like you to lift your skirt…"

Dan's mouth dropped open and James immediately protested. "Dad, what on earth are you doing?"

Gary turned on his son. "Shut the fuck up, James, I'm not talking to you. Now where was I? Oh yes, Daisy I would like you to lift your skirt, take down your tights and knickers and show me you have a cunt."

"Dad, please, stop this…"

"I won't tell you again James," his father warned. "Now Daisy, are you going to do as I asked? I won't touch you, I promise. All you have to do is let me see your cunt. That's all. So why don't you take off your tights for a start?"

Dan was shivering with fear. He looked to James for guidance but James seemed as frightened as he was. They both knew what was going on. There was only one explanation - James' father must somehow got wind that Daisy was not all she seemed.

James tried once more to reason with his father. "Please Dad, please don't do this. Please don't humiliate Daisy like this. You can't expect her to do what you are asking…"

"Oh but I do my boy, I do," Gary replied. "Do you want to know why? I had a visitor this afternoon by the name of Tristram…"

Dan suddenly lost control of his bladder; he could feel warm liquid running down one leg of his tights.

"…and this geezer said he was looking for his son who he thought was staying here and I said no that was not possible and then he said that his son might be dressing as a girl and calling himself Daisy so I thought well, there's only one way to find out…"

Dan wanted to run out of the room, but could not move. He had started to cry and James put an arm round him to comfort him, but they both knew the game was up.

"I'm sorry, Mr Mitchison…" Dan began hesitantly.

James clapped a hand over his mouth and said "No, Daisy, don't say a word. Don't tell him anything."

Dan moved his head to one side, away from James' hand. "Can't you see it's no use?" he whispered to James and then turned to address his father.

"I'm sorry, Mr Mitchison," he sobbed. "I should have told you. I'm a boy."

Gary's face darkened with fury. "Say that again," he said menacingly, "louder."

Dan swallowed and tried to speak louder, but he could not. "I'm a boy," he croaked.

At that moment James heard his mother's car crunch into the forecourt and the door slam as she got out. Please God, he thought, please God let her rescue us.

Gloria Mitchison walked into the charged atmosphere in the sitting room and knew immediately that something was wrong. "What's going on" she asked, looking from one face to another.

"Oh nothing much really," Gary said, trying to effect a casual manner. "Nothing much except I've just discovered that young Daisy here has got a prick between her legs and that my own son…" he began shouting "… is obviously a FUCKING FAIRY!"

Gloria sighed. She always knew it would come out one day and that it was never going to be easy when it did. "You need to calm down, Gary," she said, playing for time.

"No I don't need to fucking calm down, I need…" He paused, struck by a sudden thought. "You knew all along, didn't you? You knew from the start that this *thing*…" he gestured at Dan "… was a fucking bloke and that James was queer and you encouraged them, didn't you? You… fucking… *encouraged*… them!"

Gloria did not see any point in denying it. "If you weren't such a bloody homophobe I would have told you," she said, "but I knew you wouldn't be handle it."

Gary jumped to his feet. "You're damn right and I'm not going to handle it now." He turned towards James and Dan, who were still standing in the centre of the room. James was still holding Dan protectively. "I'm not having two fairies under my roof buggering each rotten. Fuck off out off my house, the pair of you. James, you can come back when you decide to be a man, but *you...*" he walked across to Dan and poked him in the chest "…you fucking weirdo, you fucking fake schoolgirl, I never want to set eyes on you ever again…"

"Stop this!" Gloria shouted. "You can't just throw them out."

"Oh no? Just watch me." As he made a move towards James and Dan, Gloria stepped in front of him to block his path.

"Get out of the fucking way, Gloria," he grunted.

"You're not throwing them out," she said. "He's my son, this is his home. And Daisy is his best friend."

"I am warning you, Gloria, get out of the fucking way."

"No."

James and Dan watched on with horror as Gary drew back his fist and hit his wife, hard, full in the face. She fell to the floor, blood gushing from her nose. "You'd better go," she said to her son, holding her nose with one hand and waving at him with the other, "I'll talk to you later."

James glared at his father. "I hate you," he said, spitting the words out.

Gary was entirely unperturbed. "Yes, and I hate queers and nancy boys and bum bandits. Now fuck off out of my house and take that *thing* with you."

James seemed to have found courage from somewhere. "I want you to know," he said to his father defiantly, "that I love Daisy and she loves me and we're planning to marry and there's nothing you can do about it." He turned to his mother, who was by then sitting up holding a tissue to her nose, and asked her if she would be all right. She nodded.

"Come on Daisy," he said, taking Dan's hand, "let's get out of here."

Gary watched them leave without regret. As the electronic gates opened and James drove through in his Mini, he muttered, mimicking his son's voice "I love Daisy and she loves me. Christ. She's not even a fucking she."

* * * * *

As the gates of the Rottingdean house closed behind them, James realised that he had no idea where to go and the full enormity of what had happened began to weigh upon him. Dan was sitting hunched up in the passenger seat, whimpering, still in his school uniform, with tear stains down the front of his blouse.

"It's all over, isn't it?" he said quietly, almost to himself. "We're done for."

For want of somewhere better to go, James drove up to Beachy Head, where they had walked so often, hand in hand, in happier times. When he had parked he suggested to Dan that they should take a walk. Dan nodded misera

They walked for a while in silence, each of them lost in their own thoughts, then sat on a bench overlooking the sea. "I don't know what to do," James admitted. "I feel lost, empty, powerless. My father will never, never accept us."

"Neither will mine," Dan said.

"Remember when we were talking, only a little while ago, about the future, what we were going to do and places we were going to go? It was all a dream wasn't it? It's never going to happen. We're finished."

James paused, then burst into tears. "Daisy," he sobbed, "I don't want to live without you; I *can't* live without you."

Dan started crying again. "Nor me," he wailed. "And I don't want to live if I can't be Daisy. What are we going to do?"

James shook his head; he had no idea. They sat together with their arms around each other for some time without speaking, locked in misery. Finally James looked intently into Dan's eyes and, without saying a word, inclined his head slightly towards the cliff edge. Dan knew immediately what he was suggesting. It made sense to him, it was the obvious solution, a relief, a way out, an escape. He nodded.

They stood up, clasped each other's hand, and began to run…

Brighton Argus, 26 September 2018:

TEENAGE TRAGEDY AT BEACHY HEAD

Coastguard officers recovered the bodies of two teenagers - a boy and a girl - from the rocks at the foot of Beachy Head yesterday afternoon. Mrs Florence Owen, a passer by, described what happened. "I was taking my dog out for a walk as usual and noticed these two young people sitting on the bench where I normally sit, so I took more notice of them than usual. They were huddled together and I could see they were very upset, but I did not like to interfere. Now, of course, I wish I had. Anyway, I walked on and stopped for a rest at the next bench a little bit further on. When I looked back at the young couple I saw they were standing up. I thought they had probably decided to go home, but then to my horror they started running towards the cliff edge. I shouted at them 'Stop, stop!' but I don't think they could have heard me. Then they just disappeared."

Police reported later that a preliminary post mortem indicated that the "girl", who was dressed in a girl's school uniform, was, in fact, biologically male. Their names are being withheld until the families have been informed.

Printed in Great Britain
by Amazon